LADY ELGIN

The Lady is down

BY

Francis E. Reynolds

Sarge Publications
PMB #351
P.O. Box 1200
Alpena, MI 49707-7001

ISBN: 0-9618116-5-X
SAN 666-1327

Acknowledgements:

Illustrations...
Karen Klimczak
Fran Reynolds

Sarge Publications
PBM #351
P.O. Box 1200
Alpena, MI 49707-7001

Printed in the U.S.A., Model Printing Service, Inc.
Alpena, MI 49707

In Dedication

Carrie…

Debra…

Sue…

PROLOGUE

<u>Saturday, March 3, 1860</u>
   "Mr. Speaker."
   "The chair recognizes the gentleman from Waukesha County, Mr. Hunkins."
   "Thank you, sir." A portly middle-aged man with a fringe of gray hair on a bald pate nodded to the Speaker and turned fully to the assembly of the State of Wisconsin's House of Representatives. He straightened his shoulders and gripped the sides of the podium before him. The assembly hushed as he waited to speak. To a man they knew of what he was to speak and to a man they waited expectantly.
   "Resolved, on this date, March 3, 1860, by the Assembly, the Senate concurring, that the Governor be, and is hereby directed to, declare war against the United States and that Brigadier General S. W. Smith is hereby appointed Commander-in-Chief of all the armies of this state, and that the Glover Rescue and the Dannan Monument Funds be and are hereby placed at the disposal of the aforesaid General Smith for the purpose of putting an army on war footing."

* * *

<u>Thursday, March 15, 1860</u>
   Garret Barry leaned over the candle atop his desk cabinet and drew breaths from his cigar. He picked at a fleck of tobacco from his tongue tip and expelled a cloud of smoke to the ceiling.
   "What'll we do now?" a mid-thirty or so handsome, blue-eyed, red-haired boy asked with a mild Irish accent as he, too, lit a cigar from the same candle.
   "By law he is the commander-in-chief of our state militia and evidently has the right to disband us as a military force as he sees fit."

"Because we will not join him in his fanatic cause of secession and accept his radical views as abolitionist?" asked Fergus Kilbane, a fellow member of Barry's Union Guards and now angry at the State of Wisconsin's Governor Randall.

"He is the governor and has the state constitution on his side. I have written to him of my feelings as well as our organization but he has ordered that we surrender our arms to Colonel Rufus King and his Iron Brigade, and that I have been discharged of my commission and now I am a private citizen."

"But we can still remain a militia," noted the third member of the group, Andrew O'Connor, a middle-aged gray-haired leprechaun of a man, as he fanned the air with his cap.

"Oh, yes. We have that right as citizens to band together for the common good. But we must give up our arms as they belong to the state," Garret informed the nodding understanding fellow.

"Why not buy our own arms? We have the right as citizens to bear arms. Our own!" Andrew stated emphatically.

"Yes, that is true," Fergus agreed as he tapped the ash from his cigar into a spitoon. "But it will cost and I know of no one with a supply large enough to meet our needs. There are eighty-seven of us, all trained in the use of a rifle."

Captain Garret Barry, former commander of Barry's Union Guards, studied the glowing tip of his cigar. "I've heard some rumors. Let me think on what has transpired these past few days. I have an idea." He paused. "Give me time. I'm sure we will be able to come up with something."

CHAPTER ONE

Thursday, August 17, 1860

The afternoon sun in mid-August, a brilliant orb in a crystal-clear sky, sparkled the waters of the Straits of Mackinac between Lake Huron and Lake Michigan. The surface of the waters moved under a western wind bringing warmth of the late summer build-up of distant clouds on the horizon to be later in the afternoon a deluge of rain. Captain Henry Pratt added sugar to his fresh cup of coffee brought to him and his guest, Lieutenant George Hartsuff, by his orderly.

"It seems we are in for a bit of weather," he said, gesturing with his cup to the open window facing west from his office.

"Yes, sir," the young lieutenant agreed as he added sugar and then a splash of cream to his coffee.

"Lieutenant. This is a letter, a very private letter, that I have received from an old and dear friend of mine, Captain Garret Barry. We were in service together in Mexico in forty-eight. A braver man you will never find."

"Yes, sir," a puzzled junior officer nodded as he sat across the desk of his commanding officer, the commandant of Fort Mackinac, enjoying a cup of coffee and rolls with his captain.

"Captain Barry is now a civilian but we have kept in touch over the years. That is why l am now hearing from him." The captain paused and held an envelope in his right hand. "I...er. I hesitate a bit to go on of its contents, but I do have a sense that you may agree with what it contains, as well as a number of other things which are now coming to the fore in our national politics."

1

"Yes sir," the young officer agreed, with a nod to his captain's meaning. "I am aware, sir, as are you and many others, of the goings on at all high levels. Including the military."

"Lieutenant. I'll be honest with you and explain why I have called for this meeting." The captain rose from his chair and turned to the window that overlooked the parade grounds. "I understand that you are an abolitionist and are opposed to the introduction of slavery into the territories." He paused.

"A taken-aback lieutenant eased back in his chair.

"I am, sir. Yes, I am opposed to slavery but not to the extent of our having a civil war as some seem to contemplate. I, and I am sure you, when we served in the southern states, saw instances of slave holding that were abominable."

"And I agree, yes. My wife and I and our children pray that such shall not be perpetuated. But we still have our sense of responsibility to the Constitution and the president who sees that it is enforced."

"Yes sir."

"Lieutenant Hartsuff, I will be frank and open. You are second in command of this fort and entitled to know of events." He turned now and looked intently to the young man before him. "I have just received an order from our Secretary of War, Mr. Floyd, that any excessive or unnecessary arms are to be sent to the ordnance depot in Chicago."

A frowning lieutenant leaned forward in his chair and took a sip of his coffee.

"I also have information that other military posts in the north are to send, again, excessive or unneeded stores and ammunition to various posts and depots in the south. Chicago will only be a way station, I am sure."

"Sir. I...I don't know," a now bewildered young man sighed.

"I know. I know." The captain shook his head. "It came to me as a shock as well. But I was warned earlier by my friend Garret. He knew as early as last March that such events might be in the wind. Only the taking of the arms was by abolitionists in Wisconsin who are, or at least were, contemplating the same action as many of the southern states are now possibly engaging in. Secession! But fortunately with the nomination of Abe Lincoln for president by the Republicans they have backed off. Except that they have not replaced Garret's arms. Which brings about this letter." He handed it to the almost totally confused officer.

"He has asked me to send him any arms, rifles especially, and while he knows I would not accept any monetary rewards for such action, he would pay for the shipment and arrangements for the delivery."

The lieutenant wiped his chin and then rubbed his eyes.

"Sir. As you know, I am an abolitionist and a Democrat. Stephen Douglas is my man. He has..."

"Oh, yes. But either way. If Douglas or Lincoln are elected in November, the southern states, at least the majority of them, will secede and take with them our arms they are now having sent to them surreptitiously. But I would like us to be in this matter as equals. What is happening on the national scene is beyond you and I. If we are to do our best to preserve the union, we must act together, not as a superior to an inferior. That is the problem in our nation now. The superior and inferior thinking of some."

"Yes sir."

"Now. This letter." The captain offered an envelope to his new cohort in their subversive affairs against the orders of Secretary of War Floyd. You can read it later in more detail," he stated. "Briefly what it contains is a request for arms, rifles especially, from my friend to be able to continue his militia in Milwaukee. He had to return his arms last March and he was also discharged of his commission as a captain in the militia; he is still a captain, a retired captain of the Federal army surely, but still a captain." He sipped his coffee, then continued. "I of course as commander of this post must abide by and follow the secretary's orders. I have no choice."

"Sir," a now emboldened lieutenant with the placement of trust his captain was giving him, "just what do we have here that we must send?"

"According to the directive they have our inventory. Here is what we have that they know of," he said, handing the lieutenant a folder.

The lieutenant took it and leafed through the pages. He found the page listing the inventory. He read...two 12-pounder brass guns, two 18-pounder iron guns, two 12-pounder iron guns, two 9-pounder iron guns, five 6-pounders, one 4-pounder iron gun, 25 8/10 iron Howitzers, five brass 6-pounder field guns with carriages and limbers, one 10-inch iron mortar, 15 50-caliber Springfield rifles. He nodded in agreement from what he knew.

"It's all there and the ammunition for them," he acknowledged.

The captain smiled. "You see that they have us as having fifteen rifles?"

"Yes."

"Ah. But we have more." He paused as he again took a sip from his cup.

"More?"

"Yes. What we have is an inventory of what any artillery company would have. But remember that in the past, infantry was also stationed here. Someone evidently forgot to include them in earlier inventories after artillery units took over the post."

"Oh my God!" an astonished lieutenant gasped. "Where are they? I have never seen them."

"No. They are hidden away by our Ordnance Sergeant William Marshall."

"Bill!"

"Yes, Bill. You must remember he has been here since 1848 and has had a long succession of commandants such as ourselves, some who I am sure entrusted him to be aware of the ordnance inventory more than they should."

"Sir, I am really shocked. How long have you known of the extra rifles?" He frowned. "And how many are there?"

"According to the sergeant, forty-five."

"Forty-five! That is enough for a company, for God's sake."

"Or a militia such as my friend's."

The young lieutenant rubbed his forehead and pushed his coffee cup away.

"I don't know, sir. One or two maybe, but enough to arm... Oh."

"I agree, lieutenant, and I felt the same way when the sergeant told me..."

"He told you. When?"

"Oh, a few weeks ago. It seems he shares the same concerns that we do regarding conditions facing us today. We were discussing the concerns one day when he, as I did with you, realized that we were of the same cloth as it were."

"Where are they?"

"Let me finish," the captain stated as he offered a roll. The lieutenant shook his head. "It seems that all good things have a way of coming together. He has a son, Thomas, a sailor, who is on the *Lady Elgin* which ports here."

The lieutenant nodded, knowing.

"His son Thomas is also of the same feelings of his father and has kept in touch with the outside world, especially of events happening in the Chicago and Milwaukee areas where he has a girlfriend, an Irish lass I've been told. According to his son, the girl has a brother who is very active in the same militia group that my friend commands."

The lieutenant shook his head in wonderment.

"And where are they, you ask? The post cemetery."

"Oh, no! Not really!"

"Yes, the cemetery also houses the equipment for our winter needs. They lie under a tarpaulin covered with straw, in a shed to the rear of the property."

"What arms are they? What condition would they be in under such circumstances?"

"They are, as are the others, 50-caliber Springfield breech loaders. And their condition according to my investigation...they are fine. Oh, they'll need some attention. I am sure Captain Barry and his men will know what to do with them."

The lieutenant tapped the envelope on the desktop. "How? When?" he puzzled.

"That is one reason I have chosen to tell you of this situation as it is now coming to a head. The captain's letter, as you will see, is in reply to one I sent him informing him of the situation of our having to send arms south to arm the rebels if that is what they become, and that I have a hidden cache for his use."

"But again how? Why? How can I be of help?"

"The directive from the Secretary of the Army has asked us to place aboard the steamer *Lady Elgin* the five brass field guns with carriages and limbers noted in the inventory, and to have an officer in charge on the voyage to Chicago and turn them over to the ordnance depot there. We are to have them ready on September fifth when she sails from here. "I have posted a special letter to Captain Barry on the bark *Linda*, which left yesterday, informing him of events of the past few weeks. He will meet the shipment in Milwaukee after the dropping off of the inventoried arms in Chicago with an officer.

"Am I to be that officer? I don't see how...what of Lieutenant Smalley?"

"Yes. You will be the officer in charge but we will also include in the shipment, under separate cover, the arms for the militia. And you will also be responsible for them until delivery in Milwaukee. As for Lieutenant Smalley, I have not taken him into our confidence. I know he feels the same as we but I think we should keep this as close to ourselves as possible. Only three of us know, you, me, and Sergeant Marshall. We'll keep it that way."

The young officer rose and rubbed the back of his head and looked out over the parade grounds below to the straits beyond. He motioned with his head. "It is beginning to build up," he stated in reply to the captain's early reference to the weather conditions leading to late afternoon showers. "How will I explain this to my wife or to others?"

"You can take her with you. A spree before all hell breaks loose. As for the others, I am sure they will all know of the secretary's orders. News like that can not be hidden for its meaning."

"Sir," a now more than somber lieutenant opined, "we have any number of our men from the southern states. Private Cameron from Virginia and Private Yancy from Alabama and a few others. All fine young men but to what extent do the affairs of our country now have on their future? Whose side are they on?"

"Oh, yes, I know what you mean. Where is one's allegiance? To one's country or to one's state?" The captain too rose and finished his coffee, now cold. "Well, then. The first thing to do is to begin to make arrangements for the shipping of the arms. We have less than three weeks to prepare them for shipment."

"Sir."

"Yes."

"Sir. I was thinking. If these arms may be used against our northern forces isn't there some way we may be able to..."

"Sabotage them, as the French use the word. To make an arm unusable. I don't know. It is not for certain that all arms will reach the south. Many may stay in the north to be used by our own forces. I just don't know what to do. I suppose we must obey orders as we have been trained to do from higher-ups and hope for the best."

* * *

Fergus Kilbane, born in Derryrush, County Galway in Ireland but now a resident of Milwaukee and an American citizen, on this day his thirty-seventh birthday, entered the office of the treasurer of the County of Milwaukee as well as Garret Barry, an associate of Hiram Burke in the firm of Barry & Burke Druggists. Based on an urgent request for his presence at a meeting to be held with four others, Fergus had dropped what he was doing as a mortician and hurried to the meeting, leaving the attending to of a cadaver to his assistant.

"I would like this meeting to have been held at my home, but Mary is having a gathering of the Holy Name Society for a fund-raising for the construction needs of the new St. John's Cathedral." Garret began as Fergus now accounted for all those intended for the meeting.

Andrew F. O'Connor, a native of Numey, County Kildare in Ireland and now a tinsmith, Patrick J. Cooney of Mulrany, County Mayo, Ireland, a cobbler, Martin Sweeny, of Sneem in County Kerry, Ireland, a butcher, all now proud and proven citizens of the United States and members of Barry's Union Guards, sat about a large table upon which were placed a pitcher of beer and a bowl of pretzels.

"Gentlemen, I have called you together now as I have just received a special letter from my friend Captain Pratt in Mackinac." They all nodded, knowing of the friendship from earlier discussions.

"What he sent me is good news." He held up a beer glass as in a toast. They looked to each other and joined him.

"I also have had correspondence with our friend Congressmen Larabee who also has some good news for us. But I believe my information from Pratt will be more to our needs."

The foursome nodded and looked to each other with wide smiles and poured more beer.

"Now then," he began. "Captain Pratt informs me that he has available for us...forty-five..." he paused. "Fifty-caliber Springfield breech loader rifles already crated and awaiting delivery."

"Jaysus." Andrew expressed, blessing himself.

"I'll be damned!" Fergus exclaimed.

"God bless us," Patrick intoned.

Martin gave a belch and smiled, wiping his lips.

"According to the letter," Garret continued, "Captain Pratt will be shipping the arms on September fifth, a Wednesday. And this is interesting. They will be shipped the same time ordnance from the fort will also be sent on the same vessel to the depot in Chicago, but in two separate consignments. Our rifles are to be packed as native Indian artifacts and medicinal herbs bound for my company, Barry & Burke Druggists. That will account for their weight and size. And gentlemen... the cost is nothing except the cost of shipping. In other words, they are a donation to our cause from Captain Pratt and Ordnance Sergeant Marshall."

"Ach. That is indeed grand news but we need more than forty-five rifles," Patrick interjected.

"And that brings me to the letter from our Congressman." Garret took a long drink, letting the news sink in as each poured themselves full fresh glasses of beer. Fergus had tapped from a small keg on a table in a corner.

"He writes that he has been able to arrange for a stand of eighty Sharp's with ammunition. But instead of a donation he is asking two dollars apiece plus the shipping."

"That would cost..." Fergus figured in his mind... "one-hundred sixty dollars for the rifles alone. How much is the cost of sending and from where?"

"He didn't say where they are but the cost of shipping the lot, and he is emphatic that it is a take-or-leave it situation, is..." Garret referred to the letter... "twenty-five dollars."

"What?" Andrew burst out. "My God, where are they coming from, China?"

"Andy!" Garret said testily. Andrew shrugged at his outburst.

The captain continued, "Twenty-five dollars may seem a lot but it is a no strings offer and who are we to choose?"

"But we are getting arms from Captain Pratt," Fergus added, he, too surprised at the high shipping costs from where no one knew.

"We have not made a decision yet as to where we will get our arms," a now almost questioning Garret stated, "or even if there will be a follow-up. This could all blow up in our faces."

"You're right, of course." Patrick agreed with his captain. "As far as I can figure," he pointed with his quill pen, "it will cost us, if we include both offers, a total of one hundred twenty-five rifles and giving the shipping from Mackinac the same value, two hundred ten dollars."

"Whew! Do we need that many rifles?" Andy asked, thinking of the high cost.

"No. But we don't have them yet. How are we to know?" Patrick offered.

"As it is," Captain Barry determined, "we have a chance to be rearmed and to have extras if we enlarge our militia. The situation in the south with the nomination of Lincoln might well lead to our having possible new enlistments and... war."

"You don't think Randall will change his order to our having to give up our arms?" Fergus questioned, now sitting back and looking serious.

"No. I am afraid our governor has taken a strong stand against our receiving federal arms and who is to know if there are any arms to give with the state of events? They'll be needed by the regular army. Especially the ammunition."

The five sat in silence as the events of the afternoon began to settle in on their thinking:

Fergus Kilbane swatted at a fly and missed, almost knocking over his glass of beer down to dregs. He sighed, trying to focus his attention on the concern at hand while he had many other concerns to be taken care of and in some instances greater than trying to get arms for an almost-defunct militia he had joined with great spirit when he had become a citizen in 1853. Little did he ever dream when he left Derryrush on that beautiful spring day in 1850 as his mother and two sisters, Eileen and Margaret, called after him as he turned and waved with the sign of the cross, then passed over the hill, never to see them again, and headed on foot to Dublin in the east and eventually to America.

He finished his beer and relit his cigar that now tasted as offal, he thought. He nodded to an offer of a refill from Andy. The Hills...he remembered. Pierce and Honora and their little baby Noreen. The thoughts brought back unhappy memories he had tried to forget over the past ten years but to no avail. He only wanted to remember them as a handsome couple with a baby who had great plans for when they would be in America. Och! The *Griffith*! It had been bad enough on the *Primrose* in the passing from Liverpool to New York, but it was the *Griffith* that took their lives along with so many others. And he... he sipped his beer and took a bit of a now-stale pretzel... survived along with twenty-nine men and only one woman. He knew only one or two of them, only slightly, and the woman not at all...

"Fergus!"

"Eh? Oh yes, I was thinking." Fergus tossed the half-smoked cigar into the spittoon.

"Yes, I understand, but we must come up with some answer to both of these letters," Garret admonished as he called attention to the other equally silent and retrospect members of the group.

"I suggest we make every effort to procure the arms as presented," Garret offered as a beginning of discussion, as he swatted at flies that seemed to envelope the room.

"Two hundred ten dollars is quite a bit of money. How will we arrive at it?" Andy asked.

"We have tried lotteries before but to no great extent or profit," Patrick offered.

"And we sure as hell can't beg for the money. It would only cheapen us," Martin offered as he fanned flies from the rim of his beer glass.

Fergus stirred in his chair, his bottom getting tired of sitting. "Wait!" he almost yelled. "Ah ha! A party! A gala! An excursion! Yes, I have the answer!"

"What in the hell are you talking about?" Pat asked, surprised at Fergus's outbreak.

"Do you remember last year when the Republican Party in Racine had an excursion party from Milwaukee to Chicago when Abe Lincoln gave a tirade against Douglas?" Fergus exclaimed with enthusiasm, a broad smile on his face.

"Yes...yes, I remember," Garret answered as he recalled that at the time he would have liked to have seen Lincoln, but could not join a contingent from Milwaukee due to the illness of his son, Lil' Will, with scarlet fever.

"Ah ha!" Andy remembered, for he had wanted to see Lincoln, but he, too, could not attend. Lincoln was a Republican and Andy a Democrat, but he was interested in Lincoln's thoughts.

"Fergus," the captain said with a gleam in his eye as he saw a potential for what Fergus had come up with. "I want you to look into what you have suggested. It think it sounds great..." He paused. "Especially because I know that Stephen Douglas is to be in Chicago over the weekend of September seventh, and a parade is scheduled in his honor. Who knows? We could be in it."

"With our new arms," Andy hoped.

"That I don't know." Garret answered, now full of thoughts of how to implement Fergus's idea to the benefit of all.

* * *

The Waterbury mantel clock on the mantel of the fireplace in the office of Governor Alexander Randall of Wisconsin chimed its deep tones for three o'clock in the afternoon on August seventeenth, a warm, muggy day with the threat of a late afternoon storm. The draft in the fireplace had been opened to allow for a flow of air to draw the warm, moist air up the flue to create an air movement to try to cool the office.

The governor fanned his face with a paper fan emblazoned with a likeness of Abe Lincoln's face and the words, "The Rail Candidate 1860," then spit into a cuspidor to his right. "Damn!" he exclaimed, now wiping his brow with a handkerchief. "This has to be the hottest August afternoon that I can remember."

"Yes, it is a scorcher," agreed his partner in a game of chess, Ben Hunkin, the assemblyman from Waukesha County, and a close personal friend of the governor, as he checkmated his rival's king.

"Ah! To hell with it. It's too hot to try and concentrate," the governor groused as he pushed himself away from the card table and took a long drink of his glass of peach brandy, now warm and tasteless. "And to top it off, our ice is gone. The summer has certainly taken its toll on our ice reserves. Now what in the hell do we do?"

Assemblyman Hunkin stood and stretched, his back aching from sitting too long in a too-small armed chair for his girth. His almost daily ritual of a late lunch with his close friend and political mentor and a game or two of chess or occasionally loo could be uncomfortable, and today was one day that it was. He took his brandy glass and finished it to its last dregs. "Ah. When we have our ice, we'll wish we had our summer," he enjoined as he gathered the chess pieces, put them in a wooden box, and put it and the playing board into a drawer in a wall cabinet behind the governor's desk.

A rap on the open door to the hallway without interrupted their displeasure with the weather.

"Sir, Colonel King is here for your meeting," announced the governor's aide, a small, thin-faced fellow with a bush of blonde hair. He motioned to Colonel Rufus King, commander of the King's Iron Brigade, to enter the room.

"Ah. Colonel King. Come in. It is grand seeing you again." The governor greeted the tall, bearded figure dressed in somber black with a white starched shirt and a black bow tie. They shook hands.

"Good Lord," Ben thought as he wiped his neck and forehead with a now-soaked handkerchief. The officer, in civilian clothing, seemed almost immune to the weather. He showed almost no signs of the heat and his clothes were as trim and proper as on a cool October night. "It takes all kinds," Ben added to his thoughts as he, too, moved to greet the colonel.

"Now then, Colonel," the governor said as he gestured to a seat across the desk from him. The colonel sat stiff and crossed his right leg over his left. "Now then, what is the latest we have regarding the preparation and standard of readiness for our state militias?"

"Well, sir. Now that the threat of rebellion is getting greater everyday with the nomination of Lincoln and the splinter Democrats into their two factions, I find our militias to be ready and able to meet any demands for incorporation into Federal forces."

"Fine. Brief me," the governor said as he stepped aside to allow his aide to place a decanter of brandy on the desk between the three. He would like to have his brandy chilled as he knew Ben did, but then some liked it as is. He motioned to the colonel with a small glass, but he shook his head slightly.

"The Black Yagers and the Green Yagers are about as ready and able as they can be. They are a bit just below full companies, but we may be able to include them into other units. My main concern is that a number of them cannot speak English. They still speak their native German. They seem to be able to understand what is said or asked of them in English, but many of them cannot articulate," the colonel offered.

"Why should they?" Ben interrupted, filing his glass. "All they'll have to do is follow orders, not argue about them."

"Er...yes," Colonel King continued. "My own Iron Brigade is in fighting trim and just awaiting orders. We are at full company and armed. All three units are just awaiting orders. Our other militia..." the governor shrugged... "are still meeting, but of course, without arms. From what I hear many have lost their enthusiasm and their units are about to fall apart. That is, unless they get arms and Lincoln is elected. They were for Seward but with the split in Democrats being now north and south in leanings and Douglas hell-bent for popular sovereignty...Lincoln is their man."

"And Lincoln is no better," Ben snorted. "He is not opposed to slavery. He wants to contain slavery in its present states. A live and let live..."

"But not to allow it in the territories," the governor added.

"Oh hell! You know if Douglas wins the south stays in although they are running Breckinridge as an open gesture of rebuttal to Douglas...which may just do Douglas in, allowing Lincoln to win."

"Which means?" the governor asked, sipping his brandy.

"Which means the southern states will secede."

"Which means?" the governor asked again.

"That if Lincoln wins, we will allow Barry's Union Guards to rearm with the arms we took from them. We'll need them."

"And if Douglas wins?" the colonel now asked.

The governor took the question.

"We drop the Barry Guards and secede ourselves and declare war on the Union."

"How do you know we can get the necessary support for such action?" the colonel asked. "Only Michigan seems to agree with our stand."

"Ah, you know as well as I do that we will have the support from every state that is in the north as well as some which are the border states. It's just a matter of our getting our feelings to those such as ourselves," a now aroused governor replied.

Colonel King recrossed his legs and cupped his chin with his left hand as he tapped the arm of the chair. The grandson of a signer of the Declaration of Independence, he had very strong feelings on the thought of Wisconsin or any state of the Union seceding. But...it was not a new concept. It had almost been tried before. South Carolina in 1832 over federal tariff laws...he mulled...even the War of 1812, based on a British blockade and the unhappiness with the federal government for loss of trade with the British, roused the New Englanders to businesses but not the general public. Secession did not take place but the thought was kept.

"Colonel," the governor intoned.

"Oh, oh yes," a now attentive colonel reacted.

"Colonel. What is your feeling on our reassigning the Barry Guards as an armed unit?"

Colonel King unfolded his legs and sat forward in his chair.

"As you may know, Captain Barry and I both served in the war with Mexico. I have heard he was a brave and courageous officer. He did rile me a bit when he was first informed that you wanted his support for the state's probable secession, but I am sure that with the way events are now shaping up, he will join us if the south secedes."

"Then you feel we should wait..."

"Yes. At least until we see which way the winds blow from now till the November election."

"What if," Ben interjected, "Douglas wins?"

"As you said, he supports slavery being contained but not abolished. He then supports slavery while you abolitionists abhor it. It means war... either way."

"Damn!" The governor spat as he rose and turned to the open window overlooking a grand spread of lawn and gardens to the west. The late afternoon storm, promised earlier, was now approaching with lightning flashes and rumbles of thunder.

"What if Barry wants to get new arms?" he asked as an open question. "He could arm them. They are private citizens and can bear arms."

"I suppose he could," the colonel answered. "But it will cost money and to what degree he has any monetary resources to meet expenses, I can only guess. A good rifle costs between," he paused, "fourteen and seventeen dollars apiece. That is big money. Much more than a week's wages for most of his men. And with most of them having families...I wonder."

* * *

A crescent moon in its first quarter rising in the east was partially obscured by the now-waning storm clouds of the earlier evening storm. Stars began emerging and twinkling as the air

16

began to clear over Fort Mackinac. A refreshing west wind, now more to the north, edged the weather pattern south and east over Lake Huron.

The village of Mackinac below the ramparts of the Fort, now basking in the glow of evening twilight from the west, began its routine of the families gathering into their protective arms for the end of another August day. The evening gun on the ramparts barked and flashed... the day was done.

Sarah Jane Hartsuff shifted her position as her husband, Lt. George Hartsuff, rolled on his side and then sat upright on the edge of the bed.

"Darling?" she asked softly.

"Yes."

"Honey..." she paused. "What is bothering you? You haven't said hardly anything all afternoon. Since you were with Captain Pratt. Is there something I should know?"

"Oh, I'm sorry," he said, nodding his head. "I really am, but..."

"But what?"

"Oh, honey, I was going to talk to you about it after I had some time for my own understanding, but..."

She sat up. "Again... but what?"

The young lieutenant stood and belted his pants, looking down to his lovely wife as she lay back resting on her elbows, her nude body in soft repose in the gathering darkness of their bedroom.

"Yes... it was because of my meeting with him. He told me a few things which it now seems I am only one of three who knows of a cache of arms here on the island."

"A cache of arms? You mean hidden arms?"

"In a way. We also talked about the possibility of a secession, if Lincoln is elected, by the south or by secession of some of our northern states if Douglas or Breckinridge win. Either way, it seems to be a no-win situation for our country."

"You mean a rebellion...by the South...if Lincoln wins," a

17

now-concerned Sarah Jane said, now understanding her husband's reason for his reticence earlier.

"And that isn't all," the lieutenant added as he stepped into his boots and then struck a match, holding it to a candle on the dresser. "It seems we are to ship extra or excessive arms and other ordnance to Chicago. We have received orders from the Secretary of War, Mr. Floyd, to ship them by boat, the *Lady Elgin*, when she is here on September fifth. We are to ship whatever we have with an officer in charge." He paused. "Me."

"Oh! You."

"And you. If you wish," he added as she drew a serious look on her beautiful face.

"Captain Pratt says we can have a spree, as he called it, before all hell breaks loose."

"And can we take Cecelia? She lived in Chicago for a few years before she came to Mackinac to work at the fort as a maid and now our house servant," Sarah Jane asked, excited at the thought of getting away to Chicago.

"I suppose. It might be nice to have her with you while I tend to government business. She has been a great friend to you as well, and it will be our treat."

A now more attentive and understanding, although not totally so, Sarah Jane joined her husband in getting dressed for their dinner in the officers' mess and the Friday evening social gathering of the officers and their wives afterwards.

Sarah Jane Hartsuff, nee Tracy, was born in France, the daughter of the American consul in the City of Bordeaux. At the age of nineteen she returned with her mother to her mother's family in Albany where she, a few years later, met her future husband, West Point graduate, George Hartsuff.

They had been married upon his graduation from West Point in 1854 and spent the first three years at various bases in the south, the last year at Fort Sumter in Charleston, South Carolina, and the past three years at Fort Mackinac. Now at twenty-seven, she stood tall as a buxom lass with pale blue eyes and full ruby-red lips. The walk from their housekeeping quarters in the village to the officers' mess at the fort above the village took them on a curve of the shoreline along Huron Street which housed old-fashioned housing and businesses dating back to pre-War of 1812 days. Some were white-washed log cabins set among thickets of lilac, tall grasses, buttercups and daisies. The setting sun, now a brilliant red glow, shared its glory with the white of the fort, causing a delicate aura of pinkish tones to engulf the structure.

"Captain Pratt has asked me not to discuss our situation with any of the other officers," George continued his explanation of events as they made the turn unto Fort Street and approached the long ramp to the fort above.

"He knows they will learn of the cache soon enough when the rifles are brought out and we recrate them as Indian artifacts and medicinal herbs. But by then we should have them ready for the *Lady Elgin* on the fifth. "

"Can they be trusted?" Sarah Jane asked as she stepped aside to let an Indian couple pass carrying a fishing net between them as they headed for the water's edge and a group of others who were preparing boats for fishing.

"He seems to think so. All of our officers and most of our enlisted men were born in the north or Europe. We know of only two enlisted men who were born in the south and he plans on sending them with a few others to St. Ignace on a detail of some sort when we load the *Lady Elgin*."

"He seems to have it all worked out?"

"Oh, yes. He has given the whole thing his full attention. He is quite taken with his friend Captain Barry and his cause. All the captain has to do is pay for the freight costs to me and he will get the rifles gratis from the captain."

Sarah Jane looked up from where they were now standing at the base of the long rampway leading to the fort above. "You know, darling," she offered, "I have loved this assignment. This beautiful and historic island. But," she paused and pretended to hitch her waist, "there is one thing I will not miss."

"What?"

"I will not miss having to climb this damn rampway to the stars almost every day."

"You know something," George laughed, "I agree. It's the pits. Come on! I'll race you to the top!"

CHAPTER TWO

Tuesday, September 4, 1860

"Captain Wilson. So good to see you. I hope you had a fine trip."

"Ah yes. It was quite uneventful and we made good time."

Captain Henry Pratt, Commandant of Fort Mackinac, greeted Captain Jack Wilson, captain of the Steamer *Lady Elgin*, as the two met and shook hands as the captain descended gangway from the *Lady*, now tied up and secure to the Astor's Wharf at the foot of Main Street in Mackinaw City. The two mingled in with the crowd of passengers embarking to enjoy the remaining late afternoon and evening until getting under way at six o'clock in the morning for the extended run from Mackinac to Milwaukee. Downbound from the Soo, the *Lady Elgin* had left there at three p.m. and made good time with the weather at its finest, arriving in Mackinac ahead of schedule by over half an hour.

The two wended their way along with the others up Main Street, then turned at Fort Street and headed for the ramp to the fort above. The late summer afternoon provided a pleasant time for the two to exchange the news and events which interested them in common. Midway up the ramp Captain Wilson paused and looked to the village below and out to the expanse of northern Lake Huron and the Round and Bois Blanc Islands which lay to the south and east. The lake surface was calm with fishing boats returning to port with their day's harvest. Two collier schooners were finishing unloading coal at a pier which helped sustain the fort and the village through what could be very severe winters as well as supplying passing steamers such as the *Lady Elgin.*

"You have a beautiful spot here, one of the grandest on the Lakes," he said, and gestured with a sweep of his right arm, encompassing Haldiman Bay and the two islands beyond.

"Yes, it is really an idyllic spot. I've been here since '57 and would hope to be able to be here for another tour of duty at least. But..."

Captain Wilson nodded in understanding. "Yes. It's something we are all deeply concerned with. We are all awaiting the election results in November to see which way the winds blow... from the South or from the North."

The two stood silent and still for a moment, then returned to their walk up the ramp. "I understand you have quite a cargo for this trip," Captain Wilson offered after a few minutes of contemplation.

"Yes. That is why I wanted to walk and talk with you alone before getting to the fort and others."

"That important?"

"Yes."

"Arms?"

Captain Pratt nodded.

"Ah yes. It is the same at Fort Wilkins and at Fort Brady. Both have given me arms, not much they told me but side arms and some rifles were to be shipped below to Chicago. I am sure you have also received the same orders." Captain Wilson stopped and gazed again to the village below now with a wider view from the higher elevation. The harbor, a half-moon configuration, was cluttered with homes and businesses nestled at the base of the cliff rising behind. The sun was low on the horizon, casting long shadows over the village.

"Then you know of our orders from the Secretary of the Army regarding the recall for arms..."

"Yes. I didn't, though, until we stopped at Fort Wilkins. Lt. Grumet informed me. He was quite upset with the order but of course had to obey. The same was true at Fort Brady. They were upset but had to obey."

"Yes. As do I."

"So they will eventually end up in Alabama... maybe."

"Maybe."

"I'm to take the arms and ammunition to Chicago. What becomes of them after that I don't know." He paused. "How much have you?"

"They want the five brass field guns with ammunition that I have. Here." Captain Pratt handed him the envelope containing the order.

Captain Wilson held the papers to the fading sun. "What are your plans for loading? We leave at nine in the morning."

"Actually I have two cargos for you," Captain Pratt answered as he took the envelope. "One of the arms as well as some much-needed Indian medicinal herbs and also some Indian artifacts that must be in Milwaukee as soon as possible."

"Indian medicines? Artifacts...?"

"Er...ah. Yes," an unsure Captain Pratt stammered, now wondering how much he might be able to tell the other. "Damn it!" he sputtered, "Captain..."

"Call me Jack."

"Eh...yes...Jack. When we were talking earlier of the coming events in our lives and those of our country...the situation with the South seceding... a rebellion... I..." He stopped wondering how much he should take Jack into his confidence and plans. "These arms are to be sent to the southern states supposedly as normal transfers, but it is well known that it is one way to strip the north of arms to supply the southern forces. All perfectly according to the Secretary's wishes. However, it is all conjecture and may not be the reason at all. Yet, there are those of us who wonder."

"Do you think I would support such conniving to aid the South in getting arms? Hell, no!" a now riled Captain Wilson exclaimed. "If I could I would deep-six all of what I have in a minute if I knew they would be used against Northern forces."

"Captain... Jack... I know you only slightly. The few times we have met have been most pleasant and I do respect you, and... I hope you do me."

"I do."

"Then I must take you into my confidence... but to a degree. I feel the less one knows of my situation with the other shipment, the better."

"You have something else that you are sending to Milwaukee, not medicines or artifacts."

A now somewhat relieved Captain Pratt nodded, "Yes."

Captain Wilson nodded his head slowly and looked into the now gathering darkness to the east over Mission Point. The sun was now below the horizon in the west reflecting from high cirrus clouds portending foul weather within the next twenty-four hours or so as best he could read the weather. He turned and looked directly into Captain Pratt's eyes. "Is what you are doing for the North and our Union's cause?"

"Yes."

"Then I will help you. I need not know all the details. How can I help?"

* * *

"According to the Press-Tribune there will be a pictorial and musical exhibition of a tour through Ireland on Friday night at the Kingsbury Hall. Do you know where that is?"

Cecelia Moran thought a moment. "Yes. It is close to where we'll be docked."

Sarah Jane continued with her reading the amusement section of the Chicago Press-Tribune issue of Friday, August 31, which had arrived by mail via the mailboat *Joy Theut* that morning. "George says we are to dock at the Walchak Wharf at the foot of Rush Street."

"Oh, yes. I know where that is," Cecelia answered in the low Irish accent of her native Mayo. "It is only a few blocks from the hall. A few minutes at the most."

"That's great!" an excited Sarah Jane said as she continued now with Cecelia in their packing their clothing for the departing of the *Lady Elgin* for Milwaukee, then Chicago, the next morning.

The vacation — spree, as she referred to the trip to Cecelia — was a time to get away and see the sights of a big city, especially since Cecelia had lived there for a number of years. Cecelia was very happy to have been asked to be with her master and mistress on what they had said was a business trip as well as a getaway for them all, short a time as it might be. She was pleased to have been asked to accompany them as she would be celebrating her twenty-eighth birthday while there and hopefully might visit with some of her old friends whom she knew worked and lived in the area of Chicago they would be in. Even if she didn't see her friends at least she was with her mistress, whom she considered as a dear friend the past two years.

Cecelia folded one of George's dress uniform shirts and placed it in a valise with other articles of clothing which she had just ironed. She looked to her mistress who was now busy also attending to packing her wares. She thought of the time two years this past April, when she and two of her friends left Chicago to be servants for some of the staff of officers and their families here in Fort Mackinac. It was so remote and far from her friends and family, but she had only intended to stay the summer season or maybe a full year, then be able to return with a dowry and be married and have bairns of her own rather than raise others. She looked to her mistress now humming a light air as she continued in her packing. Fortunately, she continued in her thoughts, she had been hired by Sarah Jane almost as soon as she stepped off the boat. What a wonderful two years it had been!

"Oh. Yes," she responded to her mistress speaking to her.

"As short a time as we will be in Chicago, I hope we can find a few minutes to be able for me to see some of the latest styles for a few new dresses I would like to have for the fall and the Christmas holidays."

"Oh, there are many shops in the area that cater to travelers. I am sure you will find just what you want."

Sarah Jane nodded as she finished packing her dress suitcase and wiped her forehead with the back of her right hand.

"It is really getting warm and there is hardly a breeze." She paused and looked out the open window of the apartment's living room overlooking a nearly-deserted Cadotte Lane as it stretched to the south in the late afternoon's heat. The indigo-blue waters of Haldiman Bay, with no seeming movement, reflected on a sunny September afternoon, bringing a stillness to the island. But clouds were building in the west.

"I do hope the weather will be well for our trip."

"We have been blessed," Cecelia said as she, too, wiped her brow. "The summer has been most pleasant. A little on the warm side, but we will want all our warm days as the fall and winter will soon be upon us."

"Aye. Indeed," Sarah Jane agreed. "But for now it is our time for getting our supper. Come, let us prepare a treat for George."

* * *

Garret Barry sat back in his chair with a large smile on his face as he looked at the cash in neat piles on his desk top. "Gentlemen. You have indeed outdone yourselves. You are to be commended. We have enough money now to meet the cost of the shipment of rifles as well as a tidy sum for other expenses."

"Aye. It is grand indeed," Andrew O'Connor added as he reached and fingered a pile of fives. "They even feel good."

"As I said. You all have done well. As in preparing for our sailing on the sixth," Captain Barry added. "Fergus, how are we set for receiving the rifles? Let us all know." He motioned to the others.

"Well. As the letter your received from Captain Pratt states, they should be arriving on Thursday about five in the afternoon. They are in rough boxing as general freight, not packed as rifles would normally be expected." He tipped his beer glass to the others, Martin Sweeny, Patrick Cooney and Andrew O'Connor. "They will seem to others as possible rifles, especially since they will be in the same shipment as the other arms, the artillery pieces. They are to look, as Captain Pratt said, as to be shipped as Indian artifacts and medicinal plants."

"Forty-five rifles will still take a lot of space," Pat Cooney offered as he took a sip of his beer.

"Yes. But fortunately the *Lady Elgin* is a big boat and from what I myself have seen of her, she can handle the load," Garret explained as he, too, took a sip from his beer glass.

"How is the transfer of the rifles to us to take place?" Marty Sweeny questioned.

Garret referred to the letter.

"A Lt. Hartsuff, George Hartsuff, is accompanying the official shipment of the armament to their destination to the ordnance depot in Chicago. He is also aware of the rifles to us and will see that we get them when the *Lady* arrives in Milwaukee. They will be stored aboard in Mackinac for easy removal once the *Lady* gets in as she still has to continue to Chicago after only enough time to load and unload passengers and cargo."

"And this is when we are to board her for our day in the big city," Marty grinned, pleased with the planning for the arrival of the rifles as well as for a gala day.

"And what a day it will be!" Fergus beamed as he drew another beer from the half keg.

"From the money, we must be having quite a crowd going." A pleased Andy pointed to the desktop.

"Yes. As best I can figure, we will be having at least three hundred join us to see Douglas...The Little Giant," Fergus added and the others nodded at the designation for their choice in the upcoming presidential elections.

"I canna believe that we are getting this many... in having such luck in getting this money," Pat Cooney said as he took a fresh glass of beer from Fergus.

"Yes. Even Tim O'Brien and Francis McCormick, our two stalwart members of the Common Council, are attending with their families," Andy added. "I see that you have a good long list of those going." He pointed to envelopes filled with responses to articles published in the Milwaukee Sentinel. "It shows that we have those who support our cause. Not all are as insane as our governor or his lacky, Hunkins, who are for secession. A lot of money is being put out for us."

"Of course you must remember," Garret cautioned the group, "this money now is not all ours. He pointed to the desktop. Most of it will pay for the fares on the *Lady* but we will still have a goodly sum, as I said before, for our own needs. Yes, we have a following and thanks be to God, it is because of the likes of you and yours."

* * *

The *Lady Elgin*, berthed at the Astor Wharf, dominated the small harbor of Mackinaw City on the late Tuesday afternoon. The only steamer in at the time, it was alongside a lumber hooker, the schooner Linda, bound for Toledo in the morning. The two colliers would be leaving for the Soo and Lake Superior ports. Captain Wilson and Lieutenant. Hartsuff, with a squad of soldiers from the fort, were in the process of bringing aboard the field guns into the fourth hold aft.

"We will load the cannon to the rear and place the rifles... er... the artifacts and medicinal herbs..." Captain Wilson smiled at his slip.

Lieutenant Hartsuff nodded in understanding.

"We will place them toward the front so that you can unload them immediately when we get to Milwaukee."

"Yes. I agree," the lieutenant approved as he stepped aside on the ramp from the wharf to the starboard hold opening to allow a number of the soldiers, now toiling as they pushed and pulled the second of the five artillery pieces up the steep ramp to gain better positioning.

"It will take a number of hours to bring all the gear aboard," Captain Wilson noted as he looked to the clock above the entranceway into the Astor Warehouse across the way, now reading 6:35 in the waning late afternoon of a warm, muggy September day.

"Aye. I am having this group replaced when we get ready to load the last three pieces and their limbers. I see they are getting a little winded from their exertions. This heat isn't helping," Lt. Hartsuff added as he studied the movement of the second field gun being inched along up the ramp. "Careful, men," he called as the pushing and pulling created a shaking of the ramp, causing it to sway as in a shiver. He motioned to a private standing to one side gasping for air to get his ass up the ramp and help with the chore. The limbers for each gun had been detached earlier to make it easier to handle each gun. The lieutenant knew the gun and its carriage weighed almost a ton and the limber with its ammunition chest, now loaded. weighed almost a ton as well.

"Lt. Hartsuff." The voice of Captain Pratt drew the lieutenant's attention as he turned and saw his captain motioning to him to join he and Captain Wilson at the edge of the dock by a piling. "I see you and your men have your hands full," Captain Pratt said as he struck a match to a Havana. "The rifles are ready and I want them aboard after dark. The least the civilians see what is going on the better."

"Yes sir. The men are having a tough go of it."

"Yes," Captain Wilson agreed, "I am sorry that the ramp is as steep as it is. But then I didn't realize that we would be loading artillery pieces." He shrugged and winced as he saw the work crew bring the gun to the main deck with a thud as it dropped from the ramp end to the deck, each of the work detail taking a break from their toil.

"Have each man have a drink on me at Foreman's Bar when they are finished," Captain Pratt said with feelings for his men.

"They have earned it." He then turned to Captain Wilson and the two moved off.

Lt. Hartsuff took off his cap and fanned it to cool his reddened face from his own exertions in helping his men. He looked to his crew. "Take a few minutes, men," he called as he checked the gun for any damage. None. "All in good order, Sergeant Faist. I am going," he motioned to the sergeant in charge of the detail, "back to the fort and get you replacements for the other guns and limbers. Captain Pratt wishes to extend his thanks for your help and wants to buy you all a round a Foreman's Bar. But!" he pointed to the sergeant. "It will be only one drink on him. I'll make arrangements for you to stop in on my way to the fort."

"Och. And thank you sir and Captain Pratt," the sergeant said with what the lieutenant knew was a Bavarian accent. "I am sure the men will enjoy it."

Turning toward the ramp, Lt. Hartsuff noticed a bulletin board which had a drawing of the *Lady Elgin* and a list of some writings alongside. He looked closer and saw that it was a description of her with information about her for the casual passenger's information as they promenaded about her decks. He read quickly...named after *Lady Elgin*, the wife of the Governor General of Canada when it was built in 1851 in Buffalo, New York... hmm... it is 250 feet in length with a beam of 33 feet and a draft of 13 feet... he knew that was quite a bit more than most side-wheelers he knew of. He read on with interest... the *Lady Elgin's* weight was 1,037 tons in which was included the weight of the Brunel Vertical Beam engines that powered her two 32-foot diameter side wheels. He turned and looked to the sponson-covered wheels... yes, indeed they were big... he continued... the top speed ever obtained was 18 knots in a run from Buffalo to Chicago in 1852. The average speed on runs now was a steady 14 knots...We should get to Milwaukee in good time, he hoped... The *Lady* has a capacity of sleeping 250 in cabins and room for 100 on the deck. He stood back and looked about and was impressed by the spanking white-and-red trim of its colors... yes, indeed, he thought... she is a great vessel and should provide for Sarah Jane and Cecelia, and me, for a pleasant vacation...if only for a few days.

"Whoops!" he exclaimed, realizing he was taking time he could not really afford. "I've got to get going!"

CHAPTER THREE

Wednesday, September 5, 1860

"Stand by!" Captain Wilson called as a fine, misty rain shrouded the *Lady Elgin* in preparation to cast off from the Astor Wharf. "It's almost nine o'clock," he said, checking his watch and then the chronometer. "You may get underway, Mr. Davis."

He stepped back, allowing First Mate George Davis to take his position to the right of the helmsman, Marvin Cole. With the pull bell cord in his right hand, he called through the open doorway of the pilot house to deck gang below on the bow to cast off the hawser, then giving the bells for the entire crew to stand by to sail. He then gave the bells for the engine room to commence engines, and the side paddle wheels began their slow turning as the hawser lines were cast off from the stern and the *Lady* began to move out from the wharf. Marvin glanced toward the boat's position in relation to the receding shore.

"Ahead slow," the captain said as the first mate rang the bells. The *Lady* trembled as the engines began their labor. "Easy as we go," he cautioned to the wheelsman as the *Lady*'s bow began to swing into the calm waters of Haldiman Bay for room to turn and begin its run to Milwaukee. The *Lady* moved in a graceful turn making a wide arc with her twin wakes receding into the mist now rising over the waters.

Captain Wilson studied the shoreline as they moved now westward away from the island. "Take her to the west-south-west...two-four-seven degrees..." he commanded softly as he looked up from the chart table to see the bow moving slowly to the direction just given, the island of Mackinac now ebbing into a blur to his right as the *Lady* moved to the west. "Half ahead," he continued. "Have the lookouts keep sharp eyes for any bateaux or fishing boats."

"Yes, sir," the first mate replied as he motioned to the messenger to go forward and check the lookouts as he then pulled the bell rope for the number of pulls necessary for the engines to run up the speed to seven knots.

The calm, gray waters of Haldiman Bay were soon commingling with the waters of the Straits of Mackinac as the *Lady* moved past the marker on Pt. LaBarbe, now seen in the rising mist as the sun shone as within a halo, the marker less than a mile away to the north.

"It's weather like this that makes it interesting to sail in these waters," the first mate said. "One minute nothing, misty and gray, and the next it can be so bright as to hurt the eyes from the reflection off the water." The *Lady* was now moving at a moderate speed, creating a rolling wash as the two side paddlewheels thrust into the waters now in the upper reaches of Lake Michigan.

"Yes it is," the captain answered as he struck a loco-foco to his pipe and took a few puffs, flicking the match out the open pilot house doorway.

Ah, yes, how well I know the weather can make this life of ours so interesting, he thought and looked ahead as the bow rose in a slow rise, then to shallow out for the next rise. He turned to the young wheelsman, a tall, well-built lad with auburn hair and a neatly-trimmed beard; his blue eyes searching the waters ahead then back to the compass bearing. Mm, yes. The captain remembered. His own youth. His own days as a wheelsman. His first as an apprentice wheelsman when he was sixteen on the schooner *Boston* out of Saginaw for two seasons. Then on the *Toledo* out of Toledo. Where else? he chuckled, where he gained his title as a Wheelsman First Class. He drew a deep pull on the pipe. Oh. Yes. His next boat was the *Monticello*, Captain Thompson. Oh, no. He remembered him well. Captain Bill

Thompson, the boat's owner and one of the strictest men I have ever known. What a taskmaster! But I did learn a lot from him. I've got to admit that. And the others...the *Baltimore*, the *Illinois*...How many? He sighed. Sailing on the lakes since I was sixteen and now I am forty... twenty-four years... about as long or longer than anyone else I know. Ah. Maybe in another year or two I can call it quits and be with Elaine and the children on a full time basis rather than on a catch-as-catch can basis as it is. Ah, the farm near Coldwater. He took another puff. To be with the family and friends and trying my hand at full time farming and growing apples on the side. Ah, yes, apples. He laughed softly. Apples, why not?

"Captain, sir." First Mate Davis interrupted his reverie.

"Er... Oh, yes," an embarrassed Captain Wilson answered.

"Sir. I've noticed a more fully rising and lowering. We are heading into some heavy weather." He pointed to the southwest off the bow. The mist was now dissipated, and low on the distant horizon a darkening of clouds foretold a squall line developing under building cumulus clouds.

"Yes, I see," the captain replied, knowing well of the situation and its possibilities. "It indeed is the weather that makes it interesting to sail in these waters," he agreed with his first mate's comment earlier.

"Should we return to Mackinac?" the first mate asked.

"No. We'll continue on. We will just have to get to the lee of Beaver Island Light and ride it out as best we can. What will be our time to the light?"

The first mate checked his watch and the chart of the area. "It is almost noon and we're about halfway there now. About twenty miles."

Captain Wilson paused and thought. "As long as there is no capping, bring up our speed. I don't want any shifting of our cargo if the weather gets heavy. If it starts capping, we will have to back off. We are heavily loaded with artillery pieces and ammunition that has to be in Milwaukee tomorrow night. They may be secure enough, but I don't want to take any chances. Alert the crew as well as the passengers for the blow and take precautions."

"Aye, Sir," the first mate answered as he handed the captain the bell pull and pointed to the messenger just returning from his earlier errand. "Notify the chief steward and the cook of the change in the weather. I'll manage the crew."

"Yes, Sir," Fred Ramsey, a thin, red-haired fifteen-year-old answered in awe as he followed the first mate out of the pilot house on another errand of importance.

* * *

"We're about as ready as we'll ever be," Fergus Kilbane said with a broad smile as he entered the office of Barry & Burke Druggists above their drug store on West Kilburn Avenue. Garret Barry stood and shook the extended right hand of Fergus as he greeted him.

"You look bushed," Garret said as he offered Fergus a bottle of Jim Beam bourbon and a shot glass.

"Ah. Yes. It is hot as hell outside and I have been on the go all day," taking the two and pouring a full double shot.

"And you say we are ready," an also smiling Garret said as he sipped from his own drink.

"As well as we'll ever be. Yes. All we need is to get aboard the *Lady Elgin* and we'll be on our way to a grand Friday in Chicago." He paused as he handed Garret a thick packet of receipts of ticket sales for the *Lady Elgin*. "We have only a few left and I know that there are those that will want them."

Garret looked at the packet. "I cannot believe that we... you and Pat and Andy and Marty, have sold almost three hundred tickets for sailing on the *Lady Elgin*, as well as for the banquet on Friday night."

Fergus nodded. "Two hundred seventy-nine to be exact and as I said, others still wanting. And," he emphasized, "all are not going to the banquet. Most seem to just want to go to support our cause but not knowing of the need for payment of the rifles and some to be part of the parade, but most, just to see it and then be able to shop in the big city and see some of the attractions. Of course the Little Giant being the main attraction with the parade and the main speaker at the banquet doesn't hurt."

"Yes. Douglas is a popular contender," Garret agreed. "A real go-getter and from next door in Illinois..." he smiled, "as is Lincoln. But with the election only two months away, many want to see him and hear his words."

"Ah. Yes indeed. And it is great that you were able to get us to march in the parade. The men are really ready, willing and able. They and their families make up most of those sailing."

Garret raised his glass in acknowledgement to Fergus's compliment. "It has given us a new lease, it seems, as to our being able to show our talents as it were."

Fergus took a sip and wiped his lips. He cleared his throat. "The rifles? They are aboard? Will we be getting them?"

Garret shrugged, looking to the window overlooking the busy avenue below with its hustling and bustling in the heat of a late afternoon. The sky to the west was now in gathering storm clouds.

"I suppose so. We have no way of knowing until the *Lady* docks in Milwaukee. But I am sure that Henry...Captain Pratt...that he will have done his best to get them aboard and to us, as he explained in his letter that he would do." He turned back to Fergus who motioned with the bottle for a refill. Garret shook his head. "He also said," he continued, "that the officer bringing the rifles is sympathetic to his...our...cause of not having to be part of the secession of Wisconsin and Michigan from the Republic." He again paused. "A lieutenant...er...ah...yes, a Lieutenant Hartsuff..." He paused and wiped his forehead.

"I do have a concern about our numbers. Can the *Lady Elgin* handle our numbers? We have almost three hundred. That is one hell of a lot of people to be brought aboard on top of what number might also be aboard.

36

Fergus rubbed his chin and looked to the ceiling. He paused. "The ticket agent did not seem to think so. In fact he was quite happy to have gotten so many customers for what might be a slow weekend. He just took the money and gave us our tickets. He even had to go into his stores to get us additional tickets."

"Well, then. We'll just have to see how things are on Thursday afternoon when the *Lady* comes in," Garret said as he placed the bourbon bottle in a closet behind his desk. "It isn't that long of a run and maybe they can accommodate us after all."

* * *

"It isn't the nicest day for one to begin a vacation, or a spree as Captain Pratt calls it, but at least we are indoors and out of the weather," Sarah Jane said as she hung up a dress in the closet in the cabin that she and Cecelia were sharing on the trip to Milwaukee and then to Chicago.

"Oh, yes. Indeed. I only hope that it will be better on my return to Chicago than it was when I came north two years ago. It was in April of the year, as you remember, and it snowed all the way up," Cecelia added as she placed her travel case under the double bed she was to share with her mistress. She stood and looked about the cabin. "This is very pleasant," she acknowledged as she viewed the double bed with its white Marseilles bedspread with its accompanying Cheval dresser and commode. The cabin she thought was of good size, not at all cramped as she thought it might have been. Oh... she remembered... the sailing from Liverpool to New York on the *Primrose* when she was but a lass with her older brother Shaughn and his wife Maureen. Och! she thought with a shiver. I suppose I will never forget the crossing. Seven weeks it was, and most of the time below decks as they said, because of the storms all the way across...Ah, Shaughn and Maureen both gone now, dying of the cholera in Detroit five years ago, where they and she had settled to find a new life in a new world. Then her moving to Chicago...

37

oh... she shook her head to try to clear her thoughts... ah, yes, well at least I have a new life with a wonderful friend in Sarah Jane... she looked to her mistress with affection... I have been blessed.

"I hope that George's accommodations are as nice as ours," Sarah Jane said as she, too, observed the cabin, nodding with a smile as to it being pleasant. "He said that as the military officer in charge of the armament being shipped, he has to stay with it as part of the regulations in shipping arms on civilian transport..." she added, having heard George and the captain talking when they came aboard earlier.

"Well, at least it is for only overnight," Cecelia said, stretching from her bending over in placing the traveling case.

"Hello! Anybody home?" George's voice called through the open doorway.

"Oh, yes, honey. We're home. Come see our beautiful surroundings," Sarah Jane answered.

George entered the cabin and hugged and kissed his wife and nodded to Cecelia who gave him a wide smile and a nod in return.

"Hey, this is very nice." He noted the lush carpeting with Irish Point laced curtains giving the cabin a close but still expansive feeling.

"And how is your berthing?" Cecelia asked, remembering the term for her quarters on the *Primrose*.

"Well, thank goodness it is only for overnight. I'm with two others of the deck crew... and I have my own cot and chamber pot. You have your double bed and commode." The three laughed at his comparison of their quarters and facilities.

"Seriously, though," George held up his right hand to calm their joviality. "I have just been told that we will be getting into some rough weather and that we should take precautions... such as to remain in our quarters until the storm... which is now on the western horizon... passes us by."

"Oh, honey," Sarah Jane said, now concerned. "What about you? We are here in a cabin. What about you? You are among the freight... the artillery... and its ammunition..."

"Oh, hell. I think it's safe enough. The hold is closed and the armament and other freight are all tied down. If it is a usual storm it should pass over and we can ride it out... I've been told that the storms at this time of the year are over in a matter of a few minutes." He took Sarah Jane's hands into his. "It is those storms of spring and in October and early November that can become quite formidable and last for days on end."

"Well, thank God it is only September," Sarah Jane quipped as she placed a pert Lubin hat trimmed in navy on her head. "How do I look?" she asked.

"You look beautiful," George said, kissing her on her left cheek. He turned to Cecelia. "May I accompany you both to lunch in the saloon before the storm hits? I understand the cuisine," he emphasized the word, "on the *Lady Elgin* is quite an experience."

Again Cecelia went into remembrance as they departed the cabin and made their way along the main deck to the dining saloon forward. Cuisine. She knew the French word meaning *to cook* and how it had taken on a meaning of something special, but what she remembered of the food on the *Primrose* was another word... the Irish word... bunya!

* * *

"What's this I hear about Barry and his Guards?" an irate Governor Randall asked of Colonel King as he was ushered into the governor's office.

"His being in the parade in Chicago on Friday?" he answered, certain that was the governor's concern.

"Yes!"

"Well, sir," the colonel answered as he sat before the desk of his commander-in-chief. "If he and his Guard have been asked to march in the parade by the parade sponsors, he has every right to march if that is what he and his men wish to do. "It might just be something to boost their morale."

"But he has no arms! What in the hell is a military parade without the marchers having arms?" the governor snapped as he poured himself a small glass of brandy and took it down in one swallow, shuddering as he did.

"True," the colonel answered, not too pleased with his being questioned on something he had no control over. "But Captain Barry's Guard does more than parade with rifles. His men are experts in various details of the march. They do quick steps, reversals, diagonals, any other antics that can be done with only a drum beat and a fife. All very well done. I have seen them myself."

"What of the other units from Milwaukee... er..."

"There are the Green Yagers and the Black Yagers, neither one really up to par as marchers, but they will be marching."

The governor turned to the sound of the wind rattling the bay window behind his desk. Trees were waving in the wind that suddenly arose as rain began streaking the pane. He returned to his guest. "I also hear that Barry has quite a crowd accompanying him."

"Yes. He has made a big effort to get as much support as he can for his guard. Barry has been said to have sold over three hundred tickets to sail on the *Lady Elgin* alone."

"Three hundred?!" the governor gasped in near disbelief.

"Well, maybe not three hundred, but I do know that a large contingent of our volunteer fire fighters as well as a large number of our police, along with many of their families, are signed up."

The governor turned again to the bay window as lightning flashed and thunder rumbled. The room now was in semi-darkness as the candelabra and candles had not been lit earlier as the storm approached with almost no warning. "These afternoon downpours at this time of year can really be a little much," he muttered. "Nothing more than just a family getaway?" he guessed aloud, back to the parade.

"Perhaps. Yes, I suppose so. It isn't every day that someone from Milwaukee can get a chance to see as popular a man as Douglas, a man who next fall might well be president."

40

The governor motioned to his aide who came into the room with a taper and lit the lamps on the governor's desk. "Do you suppose we should allow Barry to have back his...er...our arms?"

"Not really. It would just present a logistic problem to get him back the arms. I have them stored in Barlington and it would take too long to get them to him in time for the parade. He can just parade and show his marching skills."

"Ah yes. You're right... I'm sorry I was a bit peevish..."

"That is alright, sir," a now more understanding subordinate granted.

"I am sorry, Colonel...can I offer you a glass of brandy or a Havana?" He pointed to the bottle of peach brandy and a humidor of cigars on a sideboard to his desk.

"Oh, no, sir. I do not imbibe in either..."

"Good for you. No bad habits."

"Not really, sir," a smiling colonel replied as he knew the governor was now in a better mood. "Wouldn't you like to be able to see Douglas and hear of his plans?" he added as a tease.

"No. Hell, no! I know his plans," he gave the colonel a wry look as he poured himself another glass of brandy and took a sip. "I have some papers that will need researching on a treaty we had with the Potawatomis back in 1841. It seems that there are some concerns by some of our western homesteaders in Kansas with their being allowed on reservations that are supporting a splinter called Ojibways that the settlers want for themselves. I've been asked to check out some fine writings that have led to loopholes in our relations with them."

Colonel King nodded, knowing of the constant friction now being found between the homesteaders and various Indian tribes who were forced to live on reservations in Kansas and Oklahoma that the homesteaders wanted to settle on. He thought, then remembered an old saw that he had heard many years ago: "The past is prologue." Ah, yes. The Indian problems? Hell, this is only the beginning.

CHAPTER FOUR

Wednesday, September 5, 1860

"What do you make of it?"

"It looks like a bitch!"

"Aye, and it's coming straight at us." Captain Wilson looked to the compass heading, then back to the horizon. "And it's moving fast."

"Yes, sir," Marvin added as he, too, looked to the compass and to the barometer, noting the rapid drop in only a few minutes.

"Maintain our course and head into it. We have no choice if we want to get into the lee of the island." The island was only a few miles away, lying between the approaching storm and the now cautious *Lady*. "Ever been in a head-on like this?" the captain asked, squinting through the now-driving rain on the pilot house windows, causing blurring.

"Oh, yes, sir. I've been in a few. I did see a dandy of a blow in Lake Erie on the *Centala*, as an apprentice in fifty-eight, but we were able to beat around it. This one is covering the whole horizon in only a matter of a few minutes."

"I wish to hell we knew more about weather patterns in this part of the world," the captain allowed as he took another look at the barometer. He frowned, then pulled the bell pull as the *Lady Elgin*, forging ahead at thirteen knots, was throttled back to a more secure speed of seven. "Thank goodness these late summer storms last only a few minutes," he added as the *Lady* eased back.

"Yes, sir," the wheelsman agreed as he held the helm hard to the course heading, hoping to enter into the calmer waters of the protection offered by the island now just ahead in a few minutes.

"We're all secure, sir," First Mate Davis called over the din of the driving rain as he entered the pilot house, "The crew is alerted but some of the passengers think things aren't as bad as it seems and are still in the saloon having lunch."

"Oh, I'm sure Fred Rice will know what to do if it gets any worse," the captain replied as he squinted through the window. "It seems to be calming now that we are in the lee of the island, but we'll still have to take precautions." He studied the chart of the waters about the island, noting the depths. He compared them as best he could with the approaching island. "Mr. Davis. We'll drop the starboard anchor and maintain low speed as long as the storm is about us. Have the anchoring detail prepare to drop the anchor on my command."

"Yes, sir," the first mate nodded as he headed out of the doorway.

The captain turned to the wheelsman. "How are we doing?"

"We are holding," a now-struggling Marvin grunted. "It is calming a bit, but..." He glanced to his right and saw to the north the whitecaps of surging waters on Lake Michigan only less than a half-mile away, heading northeast in a fury toward Mackinac Island. "We're holding position but anchoring will keep us in line with heading into the wind."

"Yes," the captain agreed. He looked to the north and then south. "It doesn't seem to be slowing down out there. We may have to spend more time here than I would like, but I sure as hell don't want to try to pass South Fox on a day like this... it's even bad enough on a clear day." The captain looked intently to the bow and saw the anchoring detail standing by, waiting for the command to drop anchor. "How is she handling?" he asked. "We're about where I want us to be."

"We are doing fine. We're able to hold on course," Marvin answered as the bow held in line now to the approaching shore-line about a quarter mile away.

"Good!" Captain Wilson shouted as he opened the door and stood on the starboard bridge side and waved his arms in arching movements. The first mate pointed his right arm to the anchor as the holding pin was tripped and the anchor dropped into the waters. He returned and then pulled on the bell cord as the *Lady* went into idle. "We'll see how well we've done. Now's the test!" He went outside and watched as the bow of the *Lady*, still moving forward, passed over the now-gripping anchor in what the captain could best determine from the chart waters as 20 to 30 feet deep. The anchor chain line slacked, then tightened as the forward motion was corrected and the *Lady* came to a bobbing stop, then began drifting sternward. The slacked chain now tightened again as the anchor held, the chain at an angle forward in waters choppy and cresting but not to the degree that the *Lady* could not ride out the storm in relative safety in the lee of Beaver Island.

* * *

"Lieutenant Hartsuff. Sir. What'll it be?" a short, gray haired, red-faced waiter greeted the lieutenant and his wife and their maid as they entered the saloon and seated themselves at a table with two other couples.

The lieutenant was taken aback but pleased at the waiter knowing who he was but wondered how he knew. "I... er... we would like one of your lunches that we have heard that the *Lady Elgin* is noted for," he stated as he helped Sarah Jane off with her silk shawl. "But we wondered if we will have time for lunch as the weather is threatening."

"Ah, the weather. Yes. The weather is no problem. Our boat is built to sail through worse than this," the waiter informed as he wiped the table top and collected two wine glasses from earlier patrons. The *Lady Elgin* rose from a low swell and settled into its trough with her throbbing side-paddle wheels moving her through a now-rising mist with the marker on Pt. LaBarbe reflecting now in an emerging sun. The next swell rose her again in a rhythmic pattern.

The saloon was nearly full with passengers as waiters moved about with trays of food and drink. "We will each have a gin sling," he said, looking to Cecelia who he knew enjoyed an occasional one with he and Sarah Jane before their dinner. Cecelia smiled and nodded as the waiter gave a short salute and departed. "Captain Pratt," he continued, "said that we might want to try the *Lady*'s Special of sauteed walleye pike served with onions, carrots, and green peppers, all of which are in season. He says it is really great."

"Whatever you wish, hon," Sarah Jane said, as she looked about and noted that most of the passengers were relatively young, all seeming to know one another and all in a gay, festive mood. "I wonder who these people are?" she asked aside to Cecelia who gave an "I don't know" shrug.

"Excuse me," George asked, hearing Sarah Jane's question. "Pardon me," he asked of a young fellow of the two couples at the same table. "Are you some group out on an outing? You all seem to be together."

"Oh, yes, we are on our way to Chicago," the fellow in about his early thirties answered, "to see Stephen Douglas. We are members of the Marquette and Alger County Democratic parties and are interested to know of his concerns regarding the probability of secession by the southern states if he is elected, or what do we do if his nemesis, Lincoln, is elected." An excited young Democrat related, "We are in for some interesting times in these coming months." Cecelia looked to Sarah Jane who was intently listening. "We in the north, the real north," he smiled, "are anxious to know of our party's platform and who best to have in Congress to meet our trying times."

"Well, I certainly hope that we will not be having any of the concerns that seem to be taking so much of all of our times of late," answered the young woman seated across from the young man. She looked to George. "I see you are in Army uniform? A lieutenant. Are you going to see Douglas?" she continued.

"Oh, no, not really," George answered, not knowing how much he should say.

"I saw that some artillery cannons were brought aboard last evening," the other young man in the group added. "We saw some other arms that were brought aboard earlier at Fort Wilkins and later in Fort Brady in the Soo. What seems to be the reason?" a now serious fellow asked.

Damn. Why in the hell did I have to open my mouth, a now sorry George asked himself. "We are only following orders," he answered, hoping the discussion would end. "My wife and our maid are making a holiday of it. Nothing sensational," he added as the waiter returned with their drinks, giving him the opportunity to give his attention to the waiter and their order.

"We would like to order our lunch. Your sauteed walleye," he said, turning from the couples.

"Ah, Sir. I'm sorry, but the kitchen is closed for the time being. It seems that some rough weather is ahead, as you noted earlier. All we can provide you with are some sandwiches... any heavy cooking has been put on hold. We will have the walleye for our supper meal."

George looked to the two. "Oh, yes, I understand," he agreed as he looked out the window to his left and saw heavy darkness on the horizon to the south. Sarah Jane... Cecelia?" he asked.

"Well, a sandwich is better than nothing. I'm starved," Sarah Jane offered. Cecelia motioned to Sarah Jane in agreement.

"We'll each have a sandwich then. Whatever you have. I would like an ale with mine." He looked to the two again. They both shook their heads. "I'll have tea with sugar," Cecelia said. Sarah Jane nodded in agreement.

"Yes, Sir, Lieutenant Hartsuff," the waiter acknowledged as he backed off with a small salute.

How in the hell does he know my name? George wondered. I'm just one of many but he knows my name. Hmmm. That's interesting.

* * *

"The *Lady Elgin* is to arrive by five o'clock tomorrow afternoon and we can unload her of the rifles as soon as she docks," Fergus said as he sipped his beer. "Captain Pratt said he was placing the rifles forward for quick pick up as soon as she gets in. That will give us time to take them to my mortuary for storage while we are in Chicago. Aye, that should give us plenty of time to do that and still return to the boat and sail on Tuesday at seven. Och. Plenty of time." Fergus Kilbane blew a ring of smoke to the ceiling as he sat back and relaxed in his chair as Marty Sweeny filled his glass from the beer keg and motioned to Pat Cooney for his glass to refill.

"I've been told by Garret that we have sold over 300 tickets for the sailing and we should realize all of our costs for the rifles," Marty said as he handed Pat his full glass.

"Has he said anything of the rifles from Larabee? We're supposed to be getting some from him," Andy O'Connor asked, his turn for a refill.

"Yes. He said that we are to get the eighty of them for two dollars each plus the shipping," Fergus said. "We have the money for them as well. But we will not be able to get them until after being in the parade and returning here to Milwaukee. They are supposed to be in transit and won't be here until Monday or Tuesday."

"And we are to pay for them in cash, no IOU's," Marty added.

"Will the boat be able to take them all?" Andy asked, questioning the number of revelers.

"I suppose so," Fergus said, stretching. "According to the ticket agent, the latest figures show our having over 348 to board tomorrow night. Many more than Garret figured."

"Jaysus! That's a lot for a boat. We had that many and more on the *Montreal* when I came across in fifty-two and it was a terrible time. Nine weeks it was," Andy exclaimed, trying to draw a comparison.

"Ah. But the agent seems to think the boat can handle them all," Fergus added. "It's a short trip, only about six or so hours. And if the weather is kind, it should not be too trying. And I, too, remember my crossing on the *Primrose* and...my God," he emphasized, "there is no comparison. But we will just have to make do."

"What of Garret? He's not able to meet with us?" Pat asked as he finished his beer.

"He would liked to have met with us and will be with us tomorrow, but his Mary is ailing and he said that maybe only he and Li'l Will will be able to join us," Fergus explained.

"His girls?" Andy wondered.

"Johanna. Maybe? But as we all know, she is a quiet girl. It's been said she wants to be a sister. Not one for all excitement and demands to be made on an overnight to Chicago. And of the others, little Mary, Elizabeth and Sarah Marie... all too young and with their mother not up to it. Just Garret and Li'l Will."

"Well. We seem to have been able to arrange for our rifles, to get the money to pay for them, and be able to have hundreds of our supporters to go to Chicago and see the 'Little Giant' hisself. I'm proud of what we've done," Marty said as he offered his glass for a refill.

CHAPTER FIVE

Wednesday, September 5, 1860

"Mr. Beeman, you may signal the engine room to commence speed," Captain Wilson commanded softly to the second mate as the *Lady Elgin* began to drift as the starboard anchor was weighed from the bottom of its berthing for the past five hours. The severe late summer storm was moving rapidly away to the east with quieting wind and seas. Long swells from earlier turbulent waters now created a wallow as the *Lady* angled across the swell's northeast flow on her course of due south 180 degrees and her turn at the light on the south point of Beaver Island.

"The sky to the west is clear," the captain commented to Marvin, who now took over the helm from Bill Bailey, an apprentice wheelsman, who took over for Marvin to rest and relax in preparation for the long haul from Beaver Island Light downlake to South Manitou Light and then across Lake Michigan diagonally south to Two Rivers Light in Wisconsin and then to Milwaukee. "We'll have some rolling and uncomfortable passengers for awhile but we should be seeing much better weather."

"Yes, Sir," Marvin acknowledged. He looked to the chronometer and then to the heading. The west was clear but it was now a few minutes past five and in a few hours it would be dark and out on the open waters. The run between Mackinac and Milwaukee usually was between twenty and twenty-four hours but with the delay, Marvin thought, we'll be getting to Milwaukee about ten o'clock their mean time.

"Take her to south-southwest 203 degrees," the captain ordered as the *Lady* swung her bow into an approaching swell as she cleared the shelter of Beaver Island. We should be to the Manitou Light by eight o'clock. Mr. Beeman, signal for fourteen knots. We have to make up some time."

"Yes, Sir," the second mate replied as he pulled the bell cord and the *Lady* moved with her side-paddle wheels churning and her bow rising. Captain Wilson struck a loco-foco to his pipe and took a deep drag. "Messenger," he called.

"Yes Sir!" the lad answered as he stood almost at attention to his captain.

"Tell the lookouts to keep sharp eyes out for the light at South Manitou. It will be dark by then and we should be coming abeam of it by eight o'clock. I want to be dead certain that it is seen."

"Yes Sir," Freddy said as he bolted from the pilot house.

"Mr. Beeman... Mr. Cole," the captain continued. "We may be in for an unusual weather phenomenon called 'rogue waves.' Are you familiar with the expression?"

"Yes Sir." Both answered as one.

"From what I know of the situation they are waves that can follow along with the swells we are now part of. No one seems to know their cause, but they are found sometimes in seas such as we are now entering. I don't know how to prepare for them except to try to head into them as we would any other heavy seas. If we do encounter one or more of them, let us hope it will be while we still have daylight."

"Aye. I was sailing out of Calais in France for Boston three years ago when we were caught up with some off Sable Island south of Nova Scotia," offered Second Mate Matt Beeman. "It was no fun, believe me."

"I'm sure you're right. I have in all my years of sailing never been in what is said to have been a rogue storm. Close, yes, a number of times, but I'm willing to bypass a chance," Captain added as he checked the barometer. "It's rising. Good. Let's hope it stays up."

"Yes, Sir," Marvin answered as the *Lady* rose and then settled into the trough between two swells, leaning to port then righting to starboard, her bow curling water as the side paddle wheels took on the demands of an increase in power and speed.

* * *

"Oh"! Whoa! Hold it!" Sarah Jane called as the *Lady* heeled to port as she and Cecelia braced themselves. The *Lady* moved from a broadside into a more direct entry into the prevailing winds from the southwest.

"Och. I will never get used to the conniptions of a boat on the water. Oh my God. The *Primrose* ...and here I am again," Cecelia lamented. "The boat from Chicago to Mackinac and in snow all the way and now the *Lady Elgin* and in a storm and we have just left with the big lake still to cross." She and Sarah Jane held to the bedposts and braced themselves as the *Lady* made a grand turn into the wind.

The *Lady* soon settled into a more up and down movement rather than from side to side, allowing Sarah Jane to rise from her position of being beside the bed and the dresser, both bolted to the floor. "Oh, it will soon be over. I am sure the captain would not have left the safety of the island unless he knew it was well to move out," she offered. "These past hours I am sure have caused some problems with his schedule," she added as she rose and sensed a calming of the *Lady*'s movements. "There. See," she said with a sigh of relief. "We are beginning to calm. The storm is over." She reached across the bed and took Cecelia's outstretched right hand, and the two went to the doorway and looked out to the west. The sky was now soon into sunset with the rays of the setting sun casting reflections on the high cumulus clouds now moving with pillars of golden shrouds to the north-east, hell-bent for Mackinac.

* * *

"Oh. They're secure enough. I don't think we'll have to worry about them bouncing around in any bad weather," one of the *Lady*'s crewmen commented as he and Lt. Hartsuff checked the tiedowns on the cannon carriages and limbers as well as other arms and cargo.

"Yes. They seem to be pretty well tied down. I just don't want one of them, as you said, bouncing around and landing on top of me," the lieutenant said with a grin.

The crewman laughed. "The soldiers did a good job in loading. We'll have to be the ones who unload them in Chicago." He paused. "Why? Eh... why all of a sudden are there all these arms," he gestured to the arms in the compartment in the dim light of gimble lamps, "the cannons and such being sent down from Fort Wilkins and Fort Brady and now from Fort Mackinac? You'd think there is a war or something going on."

George shrugged, not too sure what to say. "Ah, yes, my good man. Maybe not a war now. We in the military are only following orders. They may be needed now in our western outposts with the large movement west of many immigrants coming to our shores in droves to fill up the spaces left by the Indians or land taken from them." He thought that answer might please the crewman.

"Eh... yeah. Maybe you're right. The only need for heavy arms up here was when we were all set to go at it with the Canadians and the British over the 54-40 or fight rigmarole. Hell... that was," he thought.. "Hell's bells, that was ten or twelve years ago," he added. The crewman then opened a porthole to allow a breath of fresh air to enter into the compartment. "But how would you use a cannon on an Indian?" He looked out on the now-calming waters. "It looks like it's clearing. Just some swells which should die down soon. We should have a good night of it."

"I hope so," George agreed. "By regulations I am to spend my time on the boat here in the compartment, except for meals with my wife and her maid while they are having a good time," he explained. While regulations did not call for such action, Captain Pratt thought it best that I be with the arms as much as possible and as long as Sarah Jane and Cecelia had a cabin and it was for only an overnight run. Why not?

"Ah. It's only for an overnight and a day. You'll still see them for your meals," the crewman opined. "I'm sure no one will harm your cannons." He again paused. "Speaking of cannons and such..." he pointed to the stacked long box-like containers covered with burlap and tied with cord.

George pretended surprise. "Oh. Those. I've heard they are Indian artifacts from the Mackinac Island and St. Ignace areas and some herbs and such that the Indians use in their medicines. Some work real well, I understand." He continued in the charade of lies now coming to be so believed. "There is a druggist in Milwaukee who uses them in his medicines and the artifacts are to go to a museum in... in..." Where in the hell would there be a museum that would want Indian artifacts? He almost laughed.

"Oh, yes," the crewman interrupted, relieving the lieutenant's consternation. "I've heard some will help but others will kill you. But they are really heavy, the soldier boys were really worn out. But then, sir, I've got to get back to my other duties. So I'll bid you good-bye. Have fun with the cannons."

George acknowledged the crewman's help with a nod and a smile. He turned and looked out the porthole. He gazed on the passing waters, the curling of the bow waves mingling with the smooth surface of the swells. His thoughts wandered back over the events of the past few weeks... to his first meeting with Captain Pratt regarding his present situation... His view out of the porthole faced to the west and at an angle to the north. Beaver Island was receding into almost a blur on the horizon.

The western sky was darkening. What does it all mean? Oh, hell, I've thought about it and talked it over and over with Sarah Jane... Captain Pratt... But do we really know what it all means? Ah. He cupped his chin in his left hand and stared out on the waters, now dark and without form, with only the throbbing sound of the paddle wheel as they made their way to the south. What if? he asked himself. What if Douglas wins? A Democrat. So is Breckinridge. What will the north do if he is elected? Ah. No. He doesn't have a rat's chance in hell... Lincoln? One of the few Republicans. A long shot. But...some Republicans are rabid about the slavery issue and Lincoln is willing to hold as is. To live and let live the present situation, but no slavery in the territories...he gave a deep sigh. Well, George. Whatever will happen, will happen, and if a war does start, or a rebellion...or whatever, you'll be in it somewhere...sometime. Sarah Jane? She'll have to go back to her mother and family. Or...maybe stay in Mackinac! Damn!

"Sir." a voice spoke softly.

"Eh...yes." George turned toward another crewman who appeared through the semi-darkness of the compartment.

"Sir. I heard you talking with Bill James. I didn't want to interrupt."

"Yes?" George questioned, wondering who the fellow was and why here? Now?

"Lieutenant Hartsuff. Sir. My name is Thomas Marshall. My father is Ordnance Sergeant William Marshall."

"Oh, yes. I've heard you are a sailor here on the *Lady Elgin*," George acknowledged, relieved. "I was wondering when we would meet."

"I know, sir. I didn't want to bother you when you were talking with Bill. My father told me yesterday of the rifle shipments being sent to a militia group in Milwaukee. I know of their need for them."

George looked more intently at the young man before him. Average height... in his early twenties, he knew... Yes. He did resemble his father with a big nose and big ears. "No one else knows?" he asked.

"No sir. Just you and me... and the captain... of course."

"Of course."

"I just wanted you to know that if you need any help... in

any way, I'll be happy to support your cause, as does my father, for the need of the militia for the rifles."

"Well thank you... Thomas... I appreciate your concern. Although I don't see any problems here on the boat. We are loaded and as soon as we get to Milwaukee, we will unload and when they are off my hands we will have done our jobs and I will spend a night and a day with my wife in Chicago and then back to Mackinac to see what in the hell happens next.

"Yes sir. I just wanted to let you know."

"And I thank you again, Tom," George said with feeling as he shook the young man's hand with a clasp and a nod.

* * *

"Captain! Captain Wilson!"

"Yes! I see it!" Captain Wilson responded to the second mate's urgent call as he joined him at the map table and looked out the facing window toward the bow, an approaching wall of grey water across the entire width of the horizon with no crest, a mound of water taller than the *Lady*'s twin stacks.

"Marvin!" Captain Wilson commanded. "Hold tight. Keep her into it! Hold!" Damn! It's too late to alert the crew and passengers, he thought, but then reflected, it is still daylight. Just! The *Lady*'s course held with Marvin and Matt both braced at the helm as the wall of water moved toward them with a deep trough in its forefront moving under the *Lady*'s dropping bow, sending spray back over the pilot house, then rose in a steep rise as the swell, a gargantuan body of slate-gray, roiling water, moved beneath her and continued its track to the northeast. "Oh my God," Captain Wilson called out as the *Lady* settled in the following trough with much calmer seas ahead. "Thank God it didn't have a crest, just a rounded hump," he called in explanation to Marvin and Matt as they both held the helm. "If it had a crest, and it will in shallower waters, if it had a crest and came down on us... eh..." he shook his head, "but we rode it out."

"Aye, we did," Matt agreed, knowing such an event as he had told of earlier. He released his hold on the helm and looked about the skyline to the west wondering if still another might be following, but all he saw was the setting sun nestling on a golden horizon.

Marvin straightened, took a deep breath, and checked the compass bearing... off three degrees he saw as he brought the bow to alignment again of southwest 203 degrees. So that was a rogue wave, he thought, thinking back to the scary event. It was bad enough in the daylight... what little we have left. What if it had been in the dark? Oh, no. He shook at the thought. Oh no.

CHAPTER SIX

Thursday, September 6, 1860

The late afternoon heat was beginning to give way to a light, freshening breeze from the northwest across the farms and forests to the west and north of Milwaukee. Thunderstorms with heavy rains, which had wracked the area for two days and nights, were now moving out to the east over Lake Michigan. A promise of fine weather for the parade on Friday was welcomed by Garret and Fergus as they met in the office of the Gordon Hubbard Co. on Farwell Avenue with Reginald Faulk, Vice President of Sales.

"I want to thank you very much for your attention to our needs," Garret said as he accepted a Havana from the humidor offered to him by the vice president.

"Oh, Sir. It is I who should be thanking you and Mr. Kilbane to have been able to have signed up so many passengers for your holiday in only a few weeks. It is quite a feat."

"Well, it is for a popular cause." He gestured to Fergus. "My number one man is the one who spent many an hour on his own to get our numbers."

Fergus, too, accepted an offered Havana. "Thank you. But it was many others... Andy... Pat... many others."

"Yes. You all certainly did. But now we will get down to brass tacks," the vice president stated as he held a candle for them to light their cigars. They both nodded a thank you. "The *Lady* is to arrive at our Jefferson Street wharf by five o'clock this afternoon." He looked at his pocket watch. "In just about four hours. I understand that many of your people are already in the neighborhood and awaiting the *Lady*'s arrival."

"Ah. Yes indeed," Fergus acknowledged. "I was just to lunch and, yes, they are in the neighborhood and all in fine fettle." He chuckled. "All the bars are full and busy."

Garret blew a cloud of smoke toward the ceiling and fanned some from his face.

"We are to have... I am to have... a shipment of Indian artifacts and medicinal plants that I must get off the boat just as soon as it arrives."

The vice president nodded in understanding. "Certainly. There will be no problem. I will give them my personal attention."

"I have had some ask if we might not be overdoing it with such numbers as we have," Fergus stated. "Can the *Lady Elgin* take as many as we have?"

"For an overnight, oh yes. The weather is pleasant now and the run to Chicago is only about six hours. The *Lady* can do that and better if she has to."

"I remember when I came over in '50 on the *Primrose* from Liverpool to New York and on the *Griffith* from Buffalo to... well..." he paused and looked for an ash tray.

"Ah yes, the *Griffith*. Who hasn't heard of her demise?" The vice president motioned to drop the ashes on the floor. "And you were on it. Only about thirty or so, I understand, survived. And you were one of those. Um."

"Yes, and that is why you can see that I am concerned as to the care and attention that will be given for our needs. The ticket seller says it is no problem."

"Oh. No need to worry," the vice president almost tut-tutted. "You must remember that ten years have passed and we in the boating business have made great strides in correcting any possible causes of a sinking or of a burning such as with the Griffith. Yes. You can rest assured that the *Lady* can handle your group's needs. " The vice president sat back in his chair, pleased at his explanation, a broad smile on his cherubic face.

"Well, gentlemen," Garret interrupted. "Our concern now is to get the people aboard at five o'clock and be on our way by seven.

We have a long night ahead of us as well as a full day tomorrow and another night to Milwaukee." He then extracted a package from a briefcase at his feet. "This is the final payment for the hauling of my goods and the artifacts. I believe it is all there."

"Thank you, Mr. Barry, for your choosing the *Lady Elgin* for your venture. I am sure we will be able to accommodate your group down and back. I almost wish I could join you, just to make the trip, as I have friends I would like to see. But for Douglas? Oh, no. I am a Republican... a radical one at that as we are sometimes called. But I do understand your wanting to see your favorite. To each his own... as the saying goes. Eh?"

"Yes, sir, I understand," a bit peeved Captain Garret Barry said as he tendered the package to the vice president. "Good day, sir."

* * *

"What do you make of it?"

"Well. They seem to have a lot of support."

"I've been told about three hundred men, women and children are going."

"The latest count is well over three hundred."

"Good God! How does he get his support?"

"He's a Catholic. His people are mainly Catholic and most of them are Irish."

"Ah. It's more than that. What of his Protestant followers?"

"I suppose it can be said that he's a very respected persona as the expression goes. He is a very popular fellow. Why else is he treasurer of Milwaukee County and superintendent of the Milwaukee post office?"

"Never mind," an exasperated Governor Randall groused. "Will he have arms... rifles?"

"I don't know. I don't think so. From what I gather, he has no arms and his militia and its followers are going to Chicago only for the day on Friday to see Douglas and be in the parade."

"Damn! Something is amiss. How can he have so much support just to be in a parade?" the governor gestured with his hands.

"I don't know," the colonel repeated.

"And what about the armaments that are supposed to be on the *Lady*?"

"My grapevine tells me arms are being brought down from a number of now-outdated forts and garrisons in the north country... the garrison in Duluth and Forts Wilkin, Brady and Mackinac. It seems to be a routine transfer of arms from one area of the country to another as the need arises," Colonel King tried to explain as best he could.

"Do you really believe that shit?"

"No sir. Not really. But I do know that an order has been sent out by the Secretary of War... Floyd and that an order from him is to be executed. Not debated or questioned. He is known for his temper."

Governor Randall turned and glared at the colonel. "Do you think for a minute that a cannon or a rifle or whatever..." he waved his arms in frustration, "is going from the Ordnance Depot in Chicago to Fort Wherever on the Whatchacallit River in Kansas Territory to shoot at Indians? Hell, they don't stand still long enough to aim a rifle at them, much less a cannon. They fight only on horseback or from ambush."

"Sir... I am just as sorry as you are and upset as well by the fact that the arms coming down on the *Lady Elgin*, and I am sure on other vessels, are going to the south. We are not at war. Yet! But the army has the right to move its arms as it sees the need. Flynn is a smart cookie, and I am sure he is within his prerogative to move armaments around the countryside as he sees fit."

"My God! Whose side are you on?"

"Sir!" a now angered Colonel King rose tall from his chair, his facial muscles twitching.

"Oh, damn it all anyway!" the governor put up his hands,

disgusted with his being upset and insulting to one of his staunchest supporters.. "Sit down." He motioned, then stood and walked to the bay window overlooking the Capital grounds. A clear blue sky rose above the green countryside, giving a peaceful grandeur to the afternoon. "I understand the storms of yesterday did quite a bit of damage in Fond du Lac." he said as an interlude in their heated discussion.

"Yes sir," a subdued but still-peeved colonel replied, knowing that quite a bit of wind damage had taken place in a number of localities around Lake Winnebago. "Sir," he continued, "we all know that our nation is going through a tremendous turmoil. We can only hope that we will be able to resolve our differences in the next election... Lincoln ...Douglas... Breckinridge... any of them I am certain has only the best interest of our nation in their hearts. We, you and I, have been born and bred in the North where such a demand for living with slavery has really never been necessary as it is in the South, at least to Southern sympathizers. Remember, slavery was allowed in all states when the Constitution was promulgated. It was a way of life in all areas then, and still in the South today." The colonel shook his head as to clear his thoughts. "My God. I never dreamed I would be saying such to you... I... I... I just don't know?"

A now contrite and truly repentant governor walked around his desk and stood before a now-shaking Colonel King. He put his right arm about the colonel's shoulders. "I am sorry. Really I am, Rufus. But you know that for the next two months our nation will be going through a bastard of a time which may well destroy our nation. Damn! I just hope we will be able to survive."

* * *

"Uh huh. We will finally get to taste the sauteed walleye that Captain Pratt raved about," George said as the three, Cecelia, Sarah Jane and he entered the saloon, the earlier bad weather now on the eastern horizon.

61

"Lieutenant Hartsuff. How nice to see you again. And ladies," an attendant greeted them attired in a red-trimmed white jacket and black pants.

George looked to the fellow. He's the waiter who took care of us earlier but now he's dressed to the nines. What gives? he wondered.

"If you will follow me I will give you a place where the three of you can enjoy your supper and perhaps a drink or two."

"Oh yes. Thank you," George replied as they followed the fellow to a table among the same group they had sat with earlier. Oh, no, he thought.

"I'll send a waiter for your order," the fellow said as he held a chair for Cecelia to be seated.

"Er...excuse me," George asked. "This is my first time on your boat and yet you know my name? How is that?"

"Ah. Lieutenant Hartsuff. My name is Fred Rice. I am the chief steward here on the *Lady Elgin*, and it is my business to know who is aboard and treat them with respect. I know that you are Lieutenant George Hartsuff and that your wife is Sarah Jane and you are traveling with your wife's maid Cecelia to Chicago."

"But earlier you were a waiter?"

"Yes. I am basically a waiter. I started out as one as a lad. But I do help out when needed, as I did earlier... I even cook on occasion and even make beds as well as wash dishes. But it is in the evenings that I tend the bar as the chief steward, as you see me now. But let me get a waiter... a real one for your orders..."

"What a guy," George said as he looked about the saloon. "I suppose it is only good business for him to do as he does. He makes someone feel important. But for now," he turned to Sarah Jane, "let's see what we will want for an appetizer drink. I think I'll have a..."

"Oh! No!" Sarah Jane shrieked as the *Lady* dropped her bow into a trough ahead of a huge mound of water moving from the southwest. She grasped Cecelia as the *Lady*, reaching the depth of the trough, staggered forward then rose in an instant as the monstrous mound swept under the hull, the paddle wheels flailing the air only to plow back into the surging waters, pulling herself along sluggishly. The *Lady* held, then bent into the afterwave as the stern lifted, the bow dropping sharply, as she surfed down the afterwave. The rising, following swell, much shallower, provided for a slowing of the forward motion and the *Lady* settled into her original course.

"Oh! I will never sail on a boat again," an almost hysterical Cecelia wailed as the *Lady* moved now in a slow, side-to-side rocking motion.

"Are you all right?" George asked the two women as he held Sarah Jane who was trembling and almost faint.

"Oh. Hon...My God! Why twice in only hours must we go through such torment?" she replied as she sat down and looked about the surroundings as the other passengers were all in the same situation. Many were holding and hugging one another, consoling each other. Some were in tears, others angry and upset.

"You'd think they would have shut down the God damn saloon!" the young Democrat spat as he helped his wife to a chair which he had righted. "They knew of this storm for hours. Why in the hell did they still let us be away from our cabins?"

"Would we have been any safer in an enclosed cabin?" another young Democrat corrected. "I'd rather be here where we saw what in hell was happening than in my cabin with a curtain over my porthole."

George knelt before Sarah Jane and tried to calm her as the other patrons gathered themselves among rumblings and anger. "We can at least thank God it happened while we still had some light," one voice called. "Let it not happen again," another added. "Oh. Look," a woman's anguished voice wailed. "Look at my dress. I spilled cocoa all over the front of it and it's ruined."

"Honey. I think the boat is settling down," George said firmly, trying to assure Sarah Jane and Cecelia, as well as himself. He rose and uprighted a chair for Cecelia who took it with a shaking head and sat beside her mistress, holding hands.

"Ladies and Gentlemen," a voice called over the now-murmuring group.

George looked up to see the chief steward entering the saloon with his hands held up, gesturing for quiet.

"Ladies...gentlemen... I am very sorry for the upset and confusion we have just gone through. But we are over it. These things happen after a heavy storm. They are called 'surge waves.' The occur after heavy swells just as we just had. There is no way of telling how severe they may be or even if there will be another one...So. Let the *Lady Elgin* treat you for any inconvenience that you may have had. The drinks are on us for the rest of the evening."

"Hey!... How about that?... Well, what do you know?" a series of calls greeted the chief steward's offer as waiters and crewmen went about lighting the lamps in the saloon and around the boat. Soon the *Lady*'s four-piece black combo began playing lively tunes and a jovial group began to enjoy themselves, keeping the waiters running.

"I'd better check the cannons and the others," George said to Sarah Jane and Cecelia when they returned to their place at the table after having attended to their needs with their cabin's commode.

"Be careful," Sarah Jane urged.

"Oh, yes, I'll take care. Things looked quite secure when I was last there. They should be all right," he said as he kissed her on her forehead and departed.

* * *

"I'm sure there will be a lot of pissed off people when we get in," Second Mate Beeman said to his relief, First Mate Davis.

"Oh, hell, yes. Whenever we get in late to someplace, we always have some who are pissed. They just don't understand what it is to sail in some of the weather we have to. Our layover at Beaver Island was a lot longer than the captain expected, as it was for all of us... but we made up for some of it," the first mate said matter-of-factly. "Let them growl."

"We just passed abeam of Port Washington Light and are holding at south-by-west, 190 degrees. We should be getting to Milwaukee at ten their mean time," the second mate informed the first mate, following procedure. "Are you ready for a long night?"

"About as much as I'll ever be. I had a good nap, so I'm ready."

"Captain said he wanted to be called when you came on. I'll give him the call... ah, here comes Marvin. He was a little tired from the run across the lake. Hey, we can get relief. A captain can't."

"Oh, hell. In the old days it wouldn't have bothered him at all," the first mate offered, wanting to defend his captain. "But he is getting older. He has been talking lately of retiring to his farm near Coldwater. He says he really misses his wife and children. Especially his Hazel, she's the one that's ailing. He's only with them in the winter months, and not always then, when he's on the Ohio or the Mississippi. Getting older? Hell, aren't we all! Keep her on 190 degrees," he instructed to Marvin who was now adjusting to the slight variation made in the transfer of the watches.

Marvin checked the compass bearing. South-by-west 190 degrees. He then took a side glance to starboard as the *Lady*, six miles offshore off Cederburg, moved south with other villages along the way showing their evening lights as beacons south to Milwaukee.

CHAPTER SEVEN

Thursday, September 6, 1860

The late afternoon sun's slanting rays cast orange reflections on the west-facing windows of the Governor's Home in Madison while great rising, billowing clouds rose high into a blue sky, foretelling more storms in the area by morning.

"What do you suppose?" Governor Randall asked of Ben Hunkin as the two stood together on the south veranda of the home. The two were taking a break from the festivities of the evening of five couples celebrating the governor's fifty-second birthday. The gathering was interrupted by a messenger with a note for the governor from Colonel Rufus King in Milwaukee. He opened and read the message. "Well now. It seems that the steamer *Lady Elgin* is to arrive this afternoon about five o'clock from Mackinac." He looked to his pocket watch. "Hmm... about now, and is loaded with arms to be placed in the Ordnance Depot in Chicago."

"The message is from Colonel King?" Ben asked, taking a draw on his Havana and then sipping his brandy.

"Yes, from Rufus." The governor looked to the telegraphed message the messenger had given him. "He says that from what he has learned, the arms aboard the *Lady Elgin* have no protection but from a single Army officer.

"So?"

"I almost believe that maybe our colonel has some second thoughts as to the final destination of those arms. He was once very adamant that we could do nothing of their destination. Either to us or to the South."

"My God! I am for our secession, but in the fall after we see the results of the election and the way our nation will go," an irate assemblyman almost raged. "Not now! What in the hell would happen if we were to stop this shipment of arms meant for the South... now legal under present military code and needs?"

"The colonel states that he has his militia in a sense of reserve."

"They have arms. Barry doesn't and the Yagers almost none. They march with gun models."

"How does he take these arms? He may have rifles... but... oh, hell, I don't know!" a now truly exasperated governor exploded.

"What in the hell are we to do?" Ben added, also exasperated.

"The messenger said he is to await our response on our thoughts and he would telegram them to Colonel King in Milwaukee. But it must be done soon, as the *Lady Elgin* is to sail for Chicago by seven o'clock. And what action will have to be done must be done in the next few hours," the governor said as he read from the message.

"Do you suppose he has plans?"

"Hell, I don't know. He must have some idea of what he wants to do."

"But whatever he has plans for, he wants your approval."

"This excursion... this getting together of people to be able to parade for Douglas... it could mean a lot of people on the *Lady Elgin*. It could... mean... a possible retaliation by some of them if we... er... King was to take control of the arms."

Governor Randall shook his head and tried to clear his thoughts. He paused and took a drink of his warm and stale brandy. Yuck! he thought. "Nor" he emphasized with a slam to the railing before him. "No, damn it. He cannot be allowed to do anything to upset our basic position of waiting until the elections in the fall. Any action now... anything brash would only lead to reaction which we are sure as hell not ready for. I'll tell the messenger to have him hold. But to take no action... I repeat... no action regarding the arms on the *Lady Elgin*."

"The soldier boys of yours did a good job in tying down the cannons and other things. They rode out the storm and the big wave real good," the crewman, Bill James, said to George as the two checked arms and other cargo in the compartment.

"Yes. And I was with them when they were brought aboard," George offered. "They really worked hard." He looked about in the dimness of the hold, the only light a lamp which a crewman held. He looked to the cannons, Withwerth six pounders. What a gun. His mind raced as he tried to figure where they may be sent, or used against who? Their use at Fort Mackinac was as single pieces on the ramparts. Were they to become a part of a battery? He reflected. What will become of me? Where will I be sent if or when a rebellion breaks out? By either side, the North or the South. My allegiance? Certainly to the Constitution and a president who will defend and enforce it. He looked to the rifles masquerading as Indian artifacts and medicinal herbs. Who will really buy it that they are not really rifles?

"Sir... I must be getting back to my duties. It is getting late and we will be preparing to get into Milwaukee. I am on the docking detail..."

"Oh. Yes." a now-attentive lieutenant answered. "Thanks. Things look very good here. They rode out the bad weather and that is the important thing." He took one last long look at the cannons. I wonder whose side you will be on. Let's hope it is on mine.

* * *

The strains of "Annie Lisle," "Jeannie With the Light Brown Hair," and "'Tis But a Little Faded Flower" contrasted to an earlier version of the bawdy "Lily Dale" as banjo strumming filled the saloon as the black combo continued the dinner hour entertainment, the diners now content and refreshed but still ready for more. The *Lady Elgin* now was abeam of Port Washington Light and was making fourteen knots an hour, moving over placid waters.

"Now. Wasn't that sauteed walleye just about the best you ever tasted?" George asked of both Sarah Jane and Cecelia as the waiter approached with a plate of mint patties and the tab.

"Yes. It was tasty. I'm glad we had the chance to try it," Sarah Jane replied with Cecelia nodding in agreement. Cecelia looked about the saloon as a number of the patrons were taking their leave to return to their cabins or promenade about the decks. She looked to the Seth Thomas wall clock on her left which read a few minutes past eight o'clock. With the delay caused by the storm, she knew they would be late in getting into Milwaukee and still later to Chicago. It has been a long day, she thought. Och. And what a day! Two storms and then the long ride across the open lake. Again her mind turned to the *Primrose*. Then in weeks across the ocean, today only in hours across a great lake. She remembered she was young and how she and the other children, when the weather was right, were allowed to go from their steerage compartments to the boat's deck and run about and enjoy a warm breeze and clear sunny skies, sometimes for only minutes, but so needed. She also remembered those who could not enjoy the freedom of the deck. Those, both young and old, who suffered from the long confinement without adequate facilities for food or drink. And the stink... Oh my God!

* * *

Darkness settled over the City of Milwaukee as the evening Angelus bells tolled to the faithful that another day had ended. To some the day did not end, but rather a continuation of events of the late afternoon at the Hubbard Wharf brought forth a gathering of many who were upset and discouraged that the *Lady Elgin* was now overdue by four hours.

"It is now after nine o'clock and we still don't know why the boat is late," said a disgruntled member of the Barry Guards, attired in full uniform of a Shamrock green tunic, trimmed with gold leaf, white pants with black boots, and topped with a green and white shako. He wiped his mustache of beer foam.

"It could well be the weather," another member said as he took a beer from a vendor. "We know the weather was bad for us these past few days. I understand that it has moved out over the lake, to the east."

"And that is where the boat is coming from," another added, "from over the lake where the storm has gone."

"Ah. Yes. But they could have had some trouble otherwise," another spoke as he looked down the docks and the streets. The Barry Guards were not alone on the now-crowded wharf and area about.

Patrick Cooney, with his wife Molly and their two bairns, John and Nora, John a thin rail of a child, six years, and Nora, a redhead of twelve, were gathered with other family members under a flickering street lamp. Other lamps along the wharf housed other members of the Milwaukee militias who were to be in the parade on the morrow, the Black Yagers with their black pointed caps and capes and gray leggings, as well as the Green Yagers similarly attired but in dark greens. To help wile away the time over most of the afternoon and into the evening, members of the city band as well as members of the militia bands played marches, lilting airs, anything to keep themselves occupied and the griping crowd amused.

"I see that some are packing up and leaving," Pat said to Andy O'Connor as they stood together and a street vendor passed them each a mug of beer.

"Yes. I heard one say... Danny O'Neil's wife Bridgit, that she didn't want to go anyway but Danny insisted. They had a spat and she left with the children. And him," Andy motioned to a young glum fellow, "he's still here."

"Aye. And," Pat looked to his wife just out of hearing, "my

Molly too is for us heading home," he said as he passed the vendor a nickel for his beer.

"Andy... Pat... I'm glad I found you," a serious Fergus Kilbane called as he joined them.

"Eh. We're just like the rest of them biding our time 'til the boat comes. What's up?" Andy answered, downing his beer.

"Garret wants to make sure all of our people are still a-holding. A number of the city band and a police unit are pulling out because of the delay of the boat coming. He wants to make sure we stay as a group."

Andy looked to Pat. Both shrugged. "Oh, hell. We'll all stay together. Is it really that bad?" he continued.

"Well, look around you. Look at those with children. They are now about done in from an already long day. But once on the boat, we all should be able to get some rest and sleep."

"Aye," Pat agreed. "But my Molly is too wondering if we should not, at least she and the children, not go. John is already missing his sleep."

"Maybe..." Andy said quizzically, "Maybe we should give ourselves... eh... another hour. And if the boat don't show we'll go and come back tomorrow if it stays for us."

"That sounds reasonable," Fergus agreed. "I'll see Garret and if he agrees, we can spread the word among our mates." He looked at his pocket watch. "It's now ten to ten. We'll wait until eleven. I'll go and tell..."

"Look!" a voice called as the others in the crowd began calling. "Here she comes!" "Yea! There's the *Lady*!" "Oh my God! Hey! It's about time!"

Fergus looked with a smile to his cohorts. "Well, I guess we are just about ready to get ourselves aboard and get some sleep."

* * *

71

"We are about abeam the Locust Street Light, Sir," First Mate Davis informed Captain Wilson who was napping in his chair in the rear of the pilot house.

"Fine," the captain replied, not really asleep but resting and still attentive to the events about him. He rose and stood beside the wheelsman Marvin. He looked to the charts of the area about Milwaukee, knowing them well but still taking no chances, especially at night. He nodded as he saw the light abeam about a mile away. "Take the *Lady* to southwest by west... 235 degrees..." He paused as the wheelsman began the turn to starboard.

"Yes Sir... southwest by west... 235 degrees."

"Keep her there until we get to the Erie Street Light."

"Mr. Davis, throttle back to seven knots." He half turned to the messenger. "Alert the lookouts that I want to go in and be able to make our turn to the wharf and want a clean shot. Mr. Davis, you may signal our intent on the whistle." A sense of excitement rose in the pilot house as the *Lady* began her approach to the entrance into Milwaukee, the lights of the city now close at hand silhouetting buildings and other structures.

"Mr. Davis," Captain Wilson said as he lit his pipe. "I have been thinking that we are going to have to make some changes in our departure time for Chicago. We are already late, so we will not do any unloading of freight due here in Milwaukee until we return from Chicago. Anything we have I am sure can wait until we return on Saturday." Even the rifles, he thought. Yes. Oh, yes. They are safe.

"Yes, Sir," an understanding first mate replied as he searched the waters about.

"We are now well over five hours into Milwaukee and I don't want to have any undue time in Chicago. Jim informed me earlier that we are below our coal reserves and will have to devote our time to getting enough on board to make our run to Chicago and back. So we will only board in Milwaukee. I want us to get to Chicago by daybreak. We'll have a long enough day there as it is," a concerned captain informed his first mate.

"Yes, Sir," the first mate agreed, having talked earlier at supper with the *Lady*'s Chief Engineer Jim Hover who had wondered of the need for the high speed and resultant using coal to the point of running low. "But," as he had stated then, "the Captain's the boss and I do as he says. He works above. I works below."

"Make ready to turn for entry, Mr. Cole," the captain said, exhaling a cloud of smoke and motioning to the first mate to take control of the bell pull. "We are on our way in. I hope we have a happy welcoming committee."

CHAPTER EIGHT

Thursday, September 6, 1860

"Good Lord! Look at that crowd," an astonished Captain Wilson let out as the *Lady* completed her docking at the Hubbard Wharf at the foot of Jefferson Street. "Where did they all come from?" he asked in general.

"I don't know," First Mate Davis offered, he, too, awed by the hundreds of people milling on the wharf and surrounding areas. Bands were playing and many in the crowd sang and jigged to the music in merriment, pleased that the long-overdue *Lady* was now docked and awaiting their boarding. "But they all seem to want to get aboard us."

"Let no one aboard unless first Class," the captain said to the purser, Steven Caryl, who had brought cargo billings for discharge in Milwaukee needing his signature, "until we know just what and who these people are. With this many I want an accounting." He turned to First Mate Davis. "I also want a priority on the loading of the coal, and I want us out of here by midnight." He looked to the chronometer. "That will give us about two hours. Put all the crew not needed for bringing aboard the passengers to helping with the coal."

"Yes sir," the first mate answered as he took leave.

"Mr. Cole...Marvin..." I want to congratulate you and Matt for your stamina in getting us across the lake. Try and get some rest. I'll use Freddy for the run to Chicago. It will give him experience and I'll call you when we get in."

"Aye, sir," a now-exhausted wheelsman agreed as he secured the helm.

An excitement arose within the captain as he stepped out on the wing of the pilot house and looked below to the sight before him in the light of the flickering lampposts. He looked then to the Hubbard Warehouse and saw Reggie Faulk making his way through the gala throng. Seeing the captain on the bridge, he waved his stovepipe hat in greeting and continued on to the now-dropped gangplank. The captain then noted that the vice president was accompanied by a number of men in green and white uniforms.

Looking again into the assemblage before him he saw others in uniform, not too distinct, but in the semidarkness, many in uniforms. Oh, yes, he remembered as he struck a loco-foco to his pipe. Oh, indeed. Tomorrow, the seventh, Friday! That is the day, yes, that is the day of the big parade for Stephen Douglas who is to give one of his great orations in Chicago. Ah, yes. These people are evidently on their way to be in the parade. Now I know the answer.

"Captain Wilson, sir. How nice it is to see you again." Reginald Faulk greeted the captain with a handshake as he and three others in uniform met with the captain in his cabin aft of the pilot house. "I trust you had a good trip... although you are late. So you must have had some adventure, eh?"

"Oh, yes, we are late and I am sorry, but we did get quite a blow above Beaver Island and I had to take safe harbor until it blew past us. But as you can see, we made it but we must be on our way again as soon as possible."

"Indeed, yes. I understand," the vice president said as he motioned to the three with him. "Captain, I would like you to meet Captain Garret Barry, the leader of one of the units that will be in the parade." He motioned to the captain who nodded.

Captain Wilson looked to a thin-faced, boyish-looking man in his middle forties with gold captain's bars sewn on the shoulders of his green tunic. The two acknowledged the introduction with a handshake. "I have heard of you, Captain, from Captain Pratt at Fort Mackinac. He sends his regards."

"Thank you, sir," Garret answered as he looked to the vice president. We cannot say too much of anything as long as he is with us. Just play it by ear, he thought.

So this is the Captain Garret of the Milwaukee Guards... also called Barry's Union Guards, the captain thought. How much does he know of what I know of his interest in the rifles? He looked sideways to the vice president. And how much does he know?

"Captain Barry," the vice president said to Captain Wilson, "has the honor of the one being responsible for the large gathering of passengers you see on our wharf. They are chomping at the bit to get aboard for Chicago for a festive time tomorrow and tomorrow night. Our main concern," he nodded to Garret, "is the care and welfare of the large number of passengers for the voyage. We know we have quite a few..."

"Oh, yes. I am amazed at the number, but I am sure we can handle them. I am having my first mate look into the boarding," the captain explained. "It is only six hours or so to Chicago and the weather has improved. I would hope we would be able to accommodate them for that time span."

"Ah, indeed," the vice president agreed. "Now that you two have met, I will take my leave and let the two of you and yours work out the details for the event. It sounds interesting, but as you may know, I support Lincoln... er... ah... yes," he stammered, realizing by the looks he received that he had overstepped. "Well, then, gentlemen. I will say adieu. Thank you, Captain Barry, for your patronage. The Hubbard Company is grateful." He made a slight bow. "Good day, sirs."

"Captain Wilson..." Garret began.

"Call me Jack. We have had too many captains... you, me, and Pratt."

"Oh, yes," a smiling Garret agreed to the much-used term among them. But then he turned serious... "Jack... I would like to unload our... my wares as soon as possible."

Jack Wilson relit his pipe. "Oh, yes. I understand... Garret... but as you know, we are being overwhelmed by your supporters...

constituents... whatever... and my crew, most of them, are now involved with the loading of a much-depleted supply of coal due to our overuse on our run from the storm at Beaver Island." He blew a cloud of smoke to the ceiling. "It is only another day. We will be able to unload the other freight, and the arms for the ordnance depot. My crew now is about exhausted and they will need a good night's sleep. I think your freight can wait until we return here to Milwaukee on Saturday."

"Yes, sir. I understand," a somewhat disappointed Garret answered. "I will talk with my people..." He paused. "I do know that Colonel King is nearby. I do not know of his plans but I am sure they will have something to do with the arms being brought from our northern outposts. He has his guard, over ninety, in reserve just a few blocks away and I am sure they are not planning to be in the parade for Douglas on Friday."

A now-subdued Captain Wilson again relit his pipe. "Do you suppose he knows of your arms... the artifacts and the medicines?"

"I don't know... No. I don't think so. He could be and I am sure is against sending the arms aboard to the depot in Chicago and further south..."

"As are we."

"And he might try something to prevent it being done."

"Damn. Your guess is as good as mine."

* * *

"Lt. Hartsuff. Sir. These are my compatriots... Fergus Kilbane, Patrick Cooney, Andrew O'Connor, and Martin Sweeny," Garret Barry stated as he introduced to the lieutenant the group as they stood aside the gangway as passengers boarded the *Lady*. "We have just left Captain Wilson who informed us that we will not be able to unload the merchandise for me due to bad timing and the need for the crew for their dire needs as well as rest."

"Yes. I understand the... er... merchandise is to stay aboard and be unloaded when we return from Chicago on Saturday. Does this cause a problem for you?"

"We really don't know," Garret stated as he looked to the rear area of the wharf where he saw the colors of the King's Iron Brigade and a stand of armed men under the command of Colonel Rufus King, standing by for orders. He pointed. "Those men are armed, we are not. We have many women and children and others not in our conspiracy. We must leave the rifles aboard and see what tomorrow or tomorrow night brings us. We will have to be prepared. We are not now."

"Then Rufus has something in mind," Fergus said as he, too, surveyed the distant gathering.

"And we're stymied," Pat Cooney added.

"Yes. We don't dare try to unload our wares. He might get ideas," Andy offered.

"Ah, yes," a now-dejected Garret agreed. "But then again, maybe it would be best that we wait until tomorrow night. The arms he knows are aboard already for the depot and will have been unloaded and we will be free and clear."

* * *

"Eh. What is it?"

"Nothing. Go back to sleep."

"What is it? Why are you being awoken in the middle of the night?"

"It's from a messenger. He just dropped off a message for me."

"A message? From who?"

"From Rufus King."

"Why? Why would he be sending you a message," she looked to the wall clock on the side wall, "after midnight?"

"Ah," a half-asleep Governor Randall lifted a candle holder as he returned to his bedroom, his wife awake and upset with an interruption of her sleep.

"He says that he is in Milwaukee and the *Lady Elgin* just left for Chicago."

"So?"

"That's what he wanted me to know."

"After midnight?"

"Yes. After midnight. All's well."

"Well, I certainly hope so," the irritated wife of the governor of Wisconsin said as she rolled over and hoped to be in the arms of Morpheus rather than her husband's which she knew he would now try to have around her.

CHAPTER NINE

Friday, September 7, 1860

"Sir. Here is a message just received from the Hubbard Warehouse," said a young fellow in the uniform of the Iron Brigade as he saluted and handed a yellow folded paper to a natilly-attired Colonel Rufus King.

"Thank you," the colonel replied with a motion of his right hand in a short salute. He turned and looked to the ranks of his men, so out of place he thought, all lined up in regimental precision while crowds of hundreds milled about them like they were out of their minds and bent on partying... but... he shook his head and looked to the message.

Col. Rufus King, Care of Hubbard Co. Warehouse
Milwaukee, Wisconsin, September 6, 1860
Do not take action on the boarding or interfering in any way
with the LADY ELGIN.
It must proceed on schedule to Chicago.
Randall

The colonel stroked his beard and frowned. He looked again to the *Lady Elgin*. There she is now, loading up somewhat subdued passengers as they filed their way aboard the boat's gangplank. The loading ramp, he saw, was up instead of usually being dropped as soon as docked. Hmm. He studied the white hull now in the glow of the yellow lamplights with the swarming of insects about them on a pleasant September night. She is literally a floating fortress, he mused. She probably has enough rifles, cannon and ammunition, as well as lesser arms, to supply a full artillery division. Knowing of the orders given by the secretary of war, to the forts to the north and in other situations in other areas of the country, it could only mean a tremendous amount of arms are being shipped south and we cannot do a damn thing about it... he thought further. Garret? He seems to be well-represented by his own guard and it seems many of their families and friends. He looked more intently at close passers-by, and recognized a number of them. What a representation, he thought. Francis McCormack of the Common Council... Sam Waegli, the register of deeds... and even the school commissioner James Rice. All Democrats, he knew, and all for Douglas.

He looked again to the telegraph message and sighed. "Sergeant Kurtze!" he commanded to Brigade Master Sgt. Donald Kurtze. "Dismiss the men. Return to your homes and families." He saluted. "Good night."

* * *

"Garret," Fergus called, pointing. "King's men are breaking ranks and seem to be leaving."

"I see. Yes," the captain answered as he and George and Fergus stood at the hurricane deck's railing overlooking the now almost-empty wharf. "He's evidently thought better than to try to do anything with the arms for the depot."

"Well, that is one hell of a relief," George added. "I don't know what would have happened. We could not really have been able to resist anything he may have done. Thank God the loading ramp wasn't down. He could have boarded from it."

"Maybe the sheer numbers of our people crowding the wharf and the gangplank together helped, along with the loading ramp not being in place," Fergus added to the assessment.

"Perhaps. Maybe we'll never know," Garret stated. "But as it is I must get to see to my son Bill and his buddy Willy... another

81

William, and get them secured for the night. He's really... they have been going all day and I am sure they could use some shut eye." He nodded, feeling the same, and added, "As could all of us. Gentlemen, I will leave you now. See you in Chicago."

"Yes, Sir," both George and Fergus answered in unison as the captain took his leave.

"And it is about time to attend to my finding my wife and her maid," George said as he gave the wharf a final look, the last numbers of people coming aboard. "Eh. Fergus... Mr. Kilbane. I am wondering if you would like to join me and my wife and her maid, if they are up to it, for a nightcap. I see the saloon is still doing a booming business," he added as they descended the stairway from the hurricane deck to the main deck and joined in with the throngs still in excitement of the excursion. "With all this commotion, I am sure they are still up."

"Why, thank you, Lieutenant... George... I could use a bit of a nip of something. It has been a long day and I am sharing a cabin with five others. I just hope I can catch a few winks later. We will all be having a busy day tomorrow and tomorrow night."

George stepped back from a capering young lass doing a jig of sorts to a flute-playing fellow in a uniform of Barry's Union Guards. Fergus laughed at the two. "That's Terry Conley and his girlfriend, Mary Duffy. They are quite a pair. A lovely couple."

"From what I have heard there is to be quite a banquet for Stephen Douglas tomorrow night," George stated as they passed on through other groupings of dancers and singing late-nighters.

"Oh, indeed. But not all of us will be attending. In fact really only a few. It is mostly for the politicians and their families. Most of us will just be in the parade or attend it and then spend the rest of the time seeing the sights of the big city and enjoying some shopping or seeing some shows early and then back to the boat for another night's ride, then home to rest all day on Sunday after Mass."

"Fergus. You are Irish?"

"Och. How can you tell?" Fergus responded with a laugh.

"Well, you do speak English quite well, not like some of our soldiers at Fort Mackinac who hail from Ireland. Many have brogues you can cut with a knife."

"Oh, yes. For some it takes time. I have been here in America these past ten years, since June. I came here to this grand land without a family tie..." He paused. "Ah, yes. A family will keep one with one's language. I see it with many of our Germans here in Milwaukee, and a number of our Irish. A family keeps old tongues still going. But," he added, "you have to remember the Irish must speak English under law. Except for the western lands of our island, most Irish speak English as the first language, even discouraging our native tongue among ourselves just to survive. I come from Galway. Most still speak Irish, but even when I was still there I could see the change..."

"Ah ha. Speaking of the Irish, here comes my wife and her maid now." George pointed down the deck through the frolicking crowd where Sarah Jane and Cecelia were making their way towards them, both smiling and laughing at the antics about them.

"Oh, George," Sarah Jane called to them with a short wave as she saw them where they stood beneath a gimbled wall lamp. "Oh, we've found you. With all these people aboard we wondered if we would ever find you. When will we be leaving?"

"It's just a matter of minutes. We may even be a little later than what the captain wanted, but I am sure we will soon be off to the big city," he said as they gave a quick hug and kiss. "The captain, I understand, has given strict instructions to his crew to get underway by midnight." He looked to his watch and then to the gangway area with only a few stragglers running at the sound of a long blast of the *Lady*'s steam whistle alerting the crew and passengers that she was getting underway. "Uh huh. Twelve-thirteen. Not too bad."

* * *

"Mr. Ramsey. I've been told by Mr. Davis that you have aspirations of someday being a wheelsman?" Captain Wilson said to Freddy Ramsey, the messenger who was all ears and attentive to the events about him in the pilot house.

The captain, with Second Mate Matt Beeman on the helm, and Freddy stood in the semi-darkness of the pilot house, the only light from the lamps about the compass housing as the *Lady* backed out slowly from the Hubbard Wharf dockage and entered into the midstream of the Menominee River. "You have seen examples of the actions taken by Mr. Beeman and Mr. Cole, as well as hearing the following of directions given to them by Mr. Davis and myself."

"Yes, Sir," Freddy replied, not really too sure what the word "aspirations" meant, but by the way the captain used the word, it must be something good. He looked to the captain who motioned to the second mate to back off and let him have access to the helm. He looked again to the captain. "Wh..." he began. He looked about him as he grasped the wheel knowing of its full importance in the maneuvering of the *Lady*. Oh, my God! he thought in awe. Oh, yes, I have wanted to be a wheelsman since I first came aboard in May...but not now! Tonight? At this time on the *Lady Elgin*? He stared at the compass before him with no heading as the second mate leaned and took the wheel and nodded as the captain gave the command "Ahead slow." He pulled the bell pull as the *Lady* moved forward. "Follow the channel lights... we are coming to the Water Street Light... we will soon be on her." Freddy gaped at the scene. Before he stood to the side of the wheelsman, Matt or Marvin, in such scenes... but now. Oh, Lord... I'm holding the wheel... er... at least Matt is steering the boat. But... oh, no... I have to pee.

"Take her to due east... ninety degrees." The captain pulled the bell pull again for an increase of speed to twelve knots as Matt nodded to the heading and stepped away as the *Lady* headed out into the open waters of Lake Michigan, leaving Freddy at the helm.

"Mr. Ramsey." His racing thoughts were interrupted by the captain. "I believe that the best experience in anything is hands-on experience. You want to be a wheelsman? A helmsman? The best way is hands-on experience. That is why now, here, in the darkness of midnight I will let you begin your instruction. You will do and follow my or Mr. Beeman's instructions and directions to the letter... or... to the degree." He paused and looked about the waters under a crescent moon reflecting on an undulating surface. "The weather, as best I can tell and with the stars and the moon above and with the use of the compass to give us our bearing, we should do well and allow our stalwart lads to get a good night's rest."

"Mr. Beeman, you may take a relief for a few hours. I will remain with our new wheelsman, Freddy? Hmm. No. From now on he is plain Fred. Freddy is a child's name. Tonight we have a young man... Fred!"

The second mate gave a stretch. "Ah, yes, Sir, it has been a long two days. I will be glad to get a rest. But Sir? What of you?"

"Oh, I'm fine, thank you. I always have an excitement in entering or leaving a port. I am fine. You can relieve me..." he looked to the chronometer... "in three hours. That way I'll be ready for our entry into Chicago, along with Mr. Cole and Mr. Davis."

Freddy...now, Fred, he corrected himself... looked intently at the illuminated compass heading of ninety degrees and was amazed at the ease that the *Lady* moved at his touch. He had seen Marvin play little games with the helm, making the *Lady* roll even so slightly from side to side without anyone ever realizing it was him and not the motion of the boat through the waters. All of this... the *Lady Elgin*... one of the largest boats on the lakes and here he was. He... Fred Ramsey of Kenosha and only a few months on the *Lady* or ever on any boat before. And now an apprentice wheelsman! Wait 'til Mom hears of this. And she wanting me to be a minister. Wow!

* * *

"Fergus... Mr. Kilbane. I would like to introduce you to my wife, Sarah Jane, and her maid, Cecelia Moran," George said as the foursome gathered together apart a bit from the now-settling down throngs. They moved to the open doorway into the saloon and found a spot they were able to find quiet enough that they could talk together.

Fergus smiled as he gave a touch of a kiss to the back of the offered right hand of Sarah Jane. He looked to her left to a tall, sedate beautiful redhead who stood poised and make no gesture for his kiss of an extended hand. Instead she smiled at him and gave a slight nod of hello, her hands clasped together at her waist. He stood tall and looked at her, their eyes meeting, she almost as tall as he. He spoke to her in his Western Galway Gaelic dialect of, "It is a pleasure to meet you. May God bless you and yours."

"Och," she replied in her Mayo Gaelic dialect, "And the same to you and yours."

"It is indeed a pleasure to meet you," he added in English, realizing they both had lost much of their native Irish with its many dialects.

"Thank you," Cecelia replied, pleased at his return to English, but happy to have been able to hear her native tongue that one could understand, not the doggerel of some of the newly-arrived recruits at Mackinac. Irish, yes. But of a bastard of English and Irish, not the native tongue. This man so...Och.

"Er...ah...yes," George interrupted, seeing a sudden interest between the two. "While it might be early for some, I feel that I must get a good night's sleep, at least what is left of the night..."

"And I," Sarah Jane agreed. "We have a long day tomorrow. Ah. Cecelia?" she asked. "I am for heading in...and you?"

"Cecelia looked to Fergus, who gave a slight shrug. "Oh, I believe I will stay up just a bit. Maybe you and your husband might like to visit for awhile."

George looked to Sarah Jane who gave him a fast nod. "Well, then. We will take our leave," he said, relieved. "You may visit as you will. We will see you both in the morning." He looked to the two who were now intent on one another. "Come on," he said as he took Sarah Jane by her right elbow. "Let's get!"

"You are from where?" Cecelia asked as they found a spot to rest.

"Derryrush. Galway. I don't suppose anyone has ever heard of it..."

"Oh!" an amazed Cecelia answered. "I have an Uncle Terrance... Terry O'Neil... who was a tinsmith who spoke highly of the people of Derryrush. I remember him speaking highly of the O'Cooneys. A name long in that area."

"Och, yes. I know the family name. It is an old name going back to the early days before the English and I am sure way before the Normans. You are a Moran from..."

"Oh, another name from way back. My people are from County Mayo, from Mulrany really. But I last lived on Achill Island before coming to America. But," she said, wondering, "how long have you been in America... the United Sates?"

Uh, he thought, what a woman. All these years and now the first really to take my attention. "I... I have been here since 1850. It is a long story..."

"Yes. Aren't they all."

"I came across from Liverpool on the *Primrose*..."

"Och! On the what?" she looked wide-eyed.

"The *Primrose*. I came to America on the *Primrose*. A boat." He wondered at her sharp reaction. "I sailed out of Liverpool on the *Primrose*."

"Oh, Fergus, Och, my God. I, too, came out of Liverpool on the *Primrose*...the same boat, but in July of 1853."

"Oh no!" Fergus exclaimed in wonder at the coincidence. "They say it is a small world... indeed. And here we are, the two of us just met, and we have between the two of us... the *Primrose*."

"Then I don't have to tell you of the crossing. The filth... the stench... the deaths." She looked aside with her eyes cast down. "I still do live it over and only hope that the conditions that I and I am sure you must have seen, are improved for those still coming and not from Ireland alone. From many lands."

"Aye," Fergus agreed, remembering... Liverpool... he rubbed his right knuckle... the *Primrose*... the canal boat... the *Griffith*... Och yes. Let us hope it all has improved. But. He took Cecelia's chin and tilted her head up. "But now! Let us think of now! Of us! It is a wonderful thing, our meeting. I do hope we will be able to visit and get to know each other. I...? You...?" Questions built up within him.

"Oh, wait." She held up her palms to calm him, now laughing at him in his exuberance in their just meeting. She gave him a coy, come-hither smile. "How do you know I am not a banshee in disguise or... or a married woman?"

"Och. But I have eyes and I can see that first you have no wedding band, and second, you are wearing a crucifix." He pointed to a silver cross that had belonged to her favorite Aunt Norine. "And no honest-to-goodness banshee would do that."

They both paused and looked at each other, both calming down to the realization that having only just met, they both in their hearts knew they were meant for each other.

* * *

"Ah. Cecelia." Sarah Jane spoke softly as she moved aside in the bed to make room for her. "It has been," she looked to the clock on the dresser, "two hours since I last saw you. How was your visit with the gentleman?"

"Wonderful. I hoped you might have slept," she said, slipping under the sheet.

"Oh, I did. For a little while at least. But with George here..."

"Och. Yes, I know."

"You and this Fergus? For two hours?"

"Oh, we had a lovely time. We just talked. He really is something special. A wonderful man. Someone like I have always wished I would find... and now..."

Sarah Jane sat up on the side of the bed. "Do you know that both George and I saw something in the two of you meeting. Two beautiful Irish personalities meeting under such tremendous odds otherwise."

"Indeed, I have dreamed of such a man. He is a little older but I am sure much more wise and settled than a younger one."

"You said you talked. He must have a story to tell," Sarah Jane asked, hunched over, excited with Cecelia's newfound happiness.

"Oh, he does indeed," a now fully-relaxed Cecelia said softly, still too excited to get to sleep. She just wanted to talk to her mistress, her very own true friend. "He is, would you believe, a mortician."

"Oh, no."

"Yes. But he came by it in an honest way."

"Oh. I am sure he did."

"Yes. He was destitute when he was in Cleveland. A boat he was on, he said it was called the *Griffith*, burned and sank just off Cleveland ten years ago. He was alone, but fortunately Cleveland had, and still has, a large Irish population and he received help. And when he was there it seemed there was a need for morticians and grave diggers and such because of a cholera epidemic as it is called, as well as the scarlet fever which killed many hundreds of people. Not just Irish but many Germans and others. All needed care and attention and because he was a learned one, he had been to school in his home village, he said one of the very few to ever finish grade school, he was able to assist a true mortician who later took him under his wing. In two years he was on his own. But he said he had a desire to travel a bit and settle elsewhere and two years later he left and ended up in Milwaukee. He said he tried Chicago, but it was too big. So now here he is one of the leading morticians in Milwaukee."

"Oh my Cecelia." A moved Sarah Jane reached for Cecelia and touched her forehead. I am so happy for you. Do you suppose...?"

"That I will return with you to the island? I..." She paused. "I really don't know. Nothing has been asked. I feel it could be a little too early for one thing. Good heavens, we just met! But if he were to ask, if he wants me, I will stay or return to him as soon as I can."

"You really feel that strongly? Both of you?"

"Of him I don't know. But we still have this day and night to get to really know one another. For me to really get to know my feelings for him."

"In one day? An evening?"

"Oh, yes. I have been many years wishing for and wanting a mate. And now I know that I have found him. Yes."

"And he?"

"I feel he feels the same. But we will give it what time we have this next day and night."

"Oh. God bless you Cecelia... and your man," a moved Sarah Jane whispered. "Now try and get some rest. You will need it."

CHAPTER TEN

Friday, September 7, 1860

"Captain Wilson, Sir. I am Major Richard Robb of the Fourth
Indiana Artillery attached temporarily to the Ordnance Depot
here in Chicago," a middle-aged officer informed Captain Wilson
with a curt salute as the two met at the base of the loading ramp
just dropped to the Walchak Wharf.

"Ah, yes, Major," the captain answered as he turned a bit to
his left. "And this is Lieutenant George Hartsuff, attached as
military officer in charge of the arms and ammunition from Forts
Wilkins, Brady and Mackinac. He will assist you and your detail."
He looked to a grouping of soldiers standing back from the
loading zone. "I must make tracks for my company's office and
report in. Good day, gentlemen."

The two officers saluted, then shook hands. "I have the list-
ings of what you have aboard," the major stated, showing his
package of inventory forms, "of what is to be delivered to me."

"Aye. And I have my lists. I am sure they will agree," George
stated. "I will have to match the two. It is required."

"If you don't mind, sir," a somewhat impatient senior officer
said testily, "I would like to unload these wares as soon as
possible. I would hope you would have the boat's crew available to help me and my men."

"I am sure you would need help, sir. But," he pointed to the
directive from the Secretary of the War, "you are to have access
to the arms directly and remove them posthaste. That means that
you and your men are to remove the arms. As you see and know,

91

the *Lady Elgin* is quite late and her crew is needed in the onloading of other cargo." As George was explaining the situation, it suddenly dawned on him of the rifles for Captain Barry and their position in front of the major's wares. Damn! he thought. How can I delay the major and still get Barry's rifles without causing a guessing game with the major or some of his men? A case of rifles looks like a case of rifles no matter how they may be camouflaged. How?

Eh. Wait! The hold! The compartment! It has two bays, starboard and port. Hell, we can unload from the other side. No, damn it! The other side is facing away from the wharf, out to the open river. Barry has nine crates all stacked neatly and ready for pickup, but what in the hell do I do with the major and his men for the time needed? Just be honest and tell him we have other items to unload before his. But I don't want too much of a delay. Oh, what the hell!

"Major, I just realized that the boat has some lesser cargo which is presently in front of your wares. They are Indian artifacts and medicines that were to have been delivered in Milwaukee last night but were not able to, due to the late arrival and almost immediate getting underway again for the captain to meet his schedule. There are a number of militia groups still on board. I will see if they may be able to move the merchandise. I am sure they will be helpful. Perhaps you and your men can take a break... breakfast?" He pointed to a restaurant up the street.

Major Robb took a side look to the lieutenant, then left down the ramp, calling his men together.

"Where in the hell can Fergus be?" George swore aloud as he looked about the wharf to the now departing crowds off for a full day of parading, shopping, sight-seeing in the big city, later entertainment and some to the banquet which, he heard, was to also honor Captain Barry.

"Aha. A fine morning to you, Lieutenant Hartsuff," a loud Fergus greeted George from behind, giving him a hearty slap on his left shoulder.

92

"Oh, Fergus! Good God! I can't believe it!" a relieved George almost exploded. "Fergus! Do I need you. And your men, now!"

"Now?" a now equally surprised Fergus asked, looking about to see what could be causing the lieutenant such consternation.

"Come." George grabbed Fergus and took him aside. "I can't go into too much detail now. But I know what it is that is in the supposed Indian artifacts and medicines that were to have been dropped off last night in Milwaukee."

"Oh," a stood-back Fergus answered, remembering then that an officer was privy.

"Just never mind. You must get your men and move the crates aside so that a detail of regular army men can begin to unload the arms destined for the depot. An army major is here with a detachment to unload and he's not too happy with the idea of using his own men as well as the delay that I have asked him to make. I just hope he will let us get to the task at hand and not get any ideas of what the cases could entail."

"I don't know," a now-serious Fergus replied. "I know that some are still aboard, and some have already gone ashore, those with families. I just saw a number of them in the saloon having coffee. I could try and..."

"Don't try... do it!" a now-demanding George urged, looking to the wharf and seeing the army detail moving off for the restaurant. Thank God, he thought. We have a little respite. "Fergus, get whoever you can. It must be done quickly!"

"Och!" Fergus sighed. "There goes my breakfast with Cecelia."

* * *

"Well then, thanks to Fergus and others who 'busted their asses,' as the good Lieutenant Hartsuff said, we have transferred the rifles to the third hold on the *Lady Elgin* and they should be safe until we return to Milwaukee tomorrow," Garret Barry said as he and others met in the dining room of the palatial Merchant's

93

Hotel on LaSalle Street. "Thank God we have had the capability of organizing our day's activities here in the dining room of the hotel. It is now ten-thirty and we are to assemble at the corner of LaSalle and Polk. We will line up on Polk's west side at twelve-thirty and be ready to parade at one o'clock." He looked to a wall clock. "Ah, we only have a little time to get ready." He looked at a schedule of the day's and evening's events. "Be sure we are all there." He then looked again to the schedule. "We are to follow behind a gathering of Douglas supporters from Whiting in Indiana. I don't know what they will be doing, but I want our militia to be in top form and to perform at our very best."

"Och. I am sure we will do our very best," Pat Cooney said, supporting his captain's wish for a grand display of their talents in the parade to be held from up LaSalle Street to the grandstand at the Water Street Pier.

"We should be able to see the sights of the big city after the parade," Andy said as he helped himself to a stale doughnut left over from the elaborate breakfast at the restaurant.

"Ah, yes. I've heard that there are many things for us to see. I want to see especially the 'Cyclorama at Kingsbury Hall. It is, I've been told, quite a picture of our Ireland, a panoramic painting," Marty said, having left Ireland when he was eight. "I want to see what a modern view would be of our Emerald Isle."

"Probably a bunch of crap," Pat offered, sipping a now-cold cup of coffee. "All I remember back in the forties was the dead along the roadside and the crowding of the poorhouses. My memories are not clean and pure as some would like to believe. But..." he wiped his chin and blinked, "but then maybe the show will present us as we were supposed to have been." He thought a moment. "Och... I too am anxious to see the presentation."

"But where is Fergus? Just as soon as we finished moving the rifles he disappeared," Andy asked, fingering another doughnut.

"You don't know?" Marty asked.

"Don't know what?" Andy looked askance.

"Och. He has met a fine young lass. He was telling me about her when he came into bed this morning. He was so excited I don't think he ever got a moment's sleep."

"Is it her what is with the wife of the lieutenant from Mackinac?" Pat entered into the conversation.

"I suppose," Marty added. "Yes. I saw the four of 'em together about the time I came to bed about one o'clock this morning. He seemed pretty happy then."

"Well, then. I am happy for our Fergus," Garret surmised as he rose to leave. "He has gone too long not to have been married and father children as he should."

"You're right," Andy agreed. "I once tried to get him interested in my wife's sister Stella, but no such. Of course her being a near midget of sorts didn't help."

"Oh, we will be seeing him shortly," Garret said. "We are to be at our point of departure by twelve-thirty," he repeated. "I am sure we all have a number of places and things to see and do before then. I myself want to take my Will and his pal to see the horses racing at Riverfront Park. So I had better move."

"And me also," Pat added. "The Missus wants the children to see the Statue of St. Malachi they have here of him. He is her favorite saint and it means a lot to her."

"Well then. I guess we will all get together at LaSalle at Polk at twelve-thirty," Andy stated as he donned his shako, giving it a rakish bent, and the foursome left for their individual concerns until the parade.

* * *

"Aye. I have until twelve-thirty to be ready for the parade. We are to gather at LaSalle and Polk. It is not too far. Just a number of blocks," Fergus said, looking to Cecelia with a deep look of love.

"Fine. We then have time to still visit and have an early lunch," she agreed as they sat in a booth of a side-street

95

restaurant off Michigan Avenue. "The time you are in the parade I can be with my mistress in her wanting to do some shopping. Fortunately the parade is in the same neighborhood. We are to meet, she and her husband, at Susan's Dress Shop on Wabash. This is their first visit to Chicago and they want to do so much in such a short time. It is well that I know the area. It will save them time." She paused and looked about the now crowded, bustling business. "They are," she continued, talking a little louder due to the increase in traffic about them, "they are on a spree, she says."

"A spree! A wild time! Boozing?" Fergus pretended shock.

"Oh, you silly arse, not a drinking spree. Just a good time." Cecelia thought a moment. "She... she has told me of the concerns of Captain Pratt, our commandant at Fort Mackinac, and of others. Yes. You and yours. The receiving of the rifles."

"Ah. Yes." Fergus nodded his head at her statement. "I didn't know quite how much you might have known about the rifles. We refer to them as Indian artifacts and medicines."

"I truly do not know too much. But I do have ears and my mistress has confided to me to a certain degree."

"Well, it is a serious matter," Fergus said as a waiter came to them with their order of ham sandwiches and ale, placing them before them. "It has to do with a very serious time in our country today. We are," he smiled and pointed his right thumb back to himself, "a nation only eighty-four years old and are in the process of possible self-destruction, with the possible secession of Wisconsin, only denied by a small majority vote when first presented to our assembly last March and now with the possible secession of a large number of southern states if Lincoln is elected." He shook his head and brushed back a forelock.

"Och. Fergus," she said, she too, shaking her head slowly. "It is indeed terrible that things are happening as they are. Slavery. The subjugation of the blacks, what ours in Ireland have seen for centuries under the English. But maybe it can be resolved without fighting among ourselves. The North! The South! Just locations but having so much meaning to those who live within their boundaries."

Fergus sat back and looked again at Cecelia. "Oh, yes, you are right. But," he sipped his ale as a relaxer, "we also have some concerns. Us! You and me!"

"Oh, Fergus." Cecelia reached across the small table and took his hands in hers. "God has given you to me. I know that he has."

"Och. My Cecelia. I, too, am sure He has intended for us to be together as one. Why else the wondrous event of our meeting under such circumstances?" He shook his head in wonder. "If and when we get to have bairns of our own, either a boy or girl first, we will call it Primrose."

"Oh, you silly arse!" she again called him, laughing at the thought of such a name for a child as she sat back and took a sip of her ale. *Our own bairn. Oh my God!*

A now more relaxed Fergus took a bite of his sandwich and chewed, thinking. "I will accompany you to where you are to meet your mistress. Then I must be off to the parade." He sat tall. "How do I look?"

"Och. You are a handsome devil. A proud rooster you are in your grand uniform. I have noticed others looking at you." She smiled. "You would make a fine soldier." She suddenly stopped at the thought. She nibbled at her sandwich' her eyes cast down.

A now-somber again Fergus looked to his sandwich and pushed it aside. "Ah, yes, a soldier. That is what I am supposed to be. A part of a militia. A State of Wisconsin agency to be used in any emergency that the governor sees the need for. In the past, Indian problems mainly. But now... but now in the event of a secession by a state from either side. It can mean only one thing. That many of us will then have to take up arms in a serious way. Not the proud marchers who can be in a parade and then go home at the end of it." He reached for and drained his ale. "Our being here in Chicago right now is only a portent of what can or will happen. The election in November. Ah, damn. They are perhaps the most important elections our nation will ever have."

"Then we must make our plans," an also-serious Cecelia stated. "If you were to be called into the active duty..." she wasn't sure of the title.

"Oh. But probably not until after the results of the election. That is still two months away."

"And of us? What until then?"

Fergus looked to her again intently. "My God, it has been only hours since I met you. And now..."

Cecelia pushed her sandwich aside and again took his hands into hers. "I can stay if you wish. I have enough clothes until my others can be sent from Mackinac."

"Yes, I would like that. But we should make plans... oh my God. I am so confused."

"As am I. Perhaps I should return with my mistress. She is quite dependent upon me. I will have to be replaced. But..." ah, yes, that word again, but, with such tremendous meaning. She gave a long sigh and released her hold of his hands. "Let us take a break... a breather. I think we both need one. You to your parade and me with Sarah Jane." She stopped and thought. Sarah Jane? I have never called her Sarah Jane aloud like that to others.

"Ah, yes," Fergus agreed. "It is getting to that time. We can meet back here."

"How long will the parade be?"

"Oh, not too long. From what Garret... Captain Barry... told us it is a relatively short route. The big occasion is the banquet tonight at the Federal Building Hall."

"You're not attending?"

"Oh, no. Not now. Besides, it is for the politicians mainly. Our Captain Barry is to be there. Only a few from our militia. Many others have their families and will be seeing the shows or just visiting. And me? My God, I'm with you!"

She smiled a warm response. "Sarah Jane and George," she now said easily, "are planning on attending a presentation by Mary McVicar, a famous actress in a play, 'The Stolen Child,' at her theater. I would like to see a... what is called a panorama painting of Ireland at Kingsbury Hall on State Street."

"Ah, yes. I know of them both. I too had hoped to see the panorama. It is called a Cyclorama. It is supposed to be quite a production. A moving scenery on large rollers, of the principal cities, public buildings, monuments, lakes, and the western mountains of Ireland. And now we can see it together and maybe relive some of our past together. We will make definite plans when the parade is over and we both return to the *Lady Elgin*. I will want to change from my uniform."

Cecelia looked to him. "Fergus, my God, I love thee," she spoke in her Mayo Gaelic.

"Fergus leaned to her and took her hands in his. "Cecelia, my God, I love thee," he spoke in his Galway Gaelic.

* * *

"Oh, hon, I am bushed. Let's rest awhile," Sarah Jane almost gasped as she reached to a small bench in the front of a leather goods and shoe store. The very dry and hot air in the mid-afternoon was beginning to take its toll on any number of excursionists from the *Lady Elgin* and other visitors to the big city. The excitement in the downtown area of the city was built around the parade at one o'clock and horse racing all day at the Riverfront Park at the end of Taylor Street. The two had wended their way leisurely through the streets taking in the sights of the largest city in the midwest of the country and enjoying their time, but for the heat.

"We really have lucked out," George said as he pointed across the avenue down half a block. "There is Susan's Dress Shop. So we have no more trudging. Now where is Cecelia?"

They were in the teeming center of the city. No air seemed to move in the crowded streets as clouds of dust and the smell of manure filled the air. There were street vendors with assorted wares and foodstuffs, as well as runners looking for visitors from out of town whom they would take to their destinations or fleece them, if such was to be the case.

"Wow! It is a hot one. I miss the winds we had on the boat," George stated. "But not the storm," he corrected as he fanned himself with his cap.

"Cecelia said she would meet us at the dress shop," Sarah Jane said, putting her right hand across her forehead to form a shadow from the glare of the sun.

"Well, we're here." George looked to a clock atop a post in front of a jewelry store two down from where they were. "It's now a little past twelve-thirty. She has time."

"Should we wait out here or go into the store?" Sarah Jane asked as she fanned herself with her purse.

"It really doesn't matter. It's hot as hell in either place. It seems to be a lot hotter here than I ever remember at Fort Sumter," George added as he stepped aside to allow a vendor pass by, pushing a cart filled with boiled corn ears. "But there it was always damp weather. Here in Chicago it seems to be so dry. At least now."

"Oh, look, there is Cecelia and Fergus," Sarah Jane called, motioning to them as they approached holding hands.

"Talk about timing," George said as he greeted Fergus with a handshake.

"My lass here really knows the town," Fergus said, motioning to Cecelia who greeted her mistress with a quick hug. "She got us here in good time."

"What are your plans?" George asked, knowing that Fergus was to leave soon to be in the parade.

"We have talked and we will meet back at the *Lady Elgin* at three o'clock," Cecelia answered, nestling close to Fergus. "This should give us much time for your shopping and the parade to run its course."

"And we will have time for the four of us to visit and have dinner together and then be off to see our own evening's entertainment," George said.

"It is a shame that the matinee at McVicker's is at three. We could meet and see it together and then we could see the Cyclorama together in the evening," Sarah Jane wondered.

"Could you miss the parade?" Cecelia asked, hoping.

"Oh, no. I am a caller. I am a count man. I am one who gives the call for a given maneuver of our motions and steps," Fergus explained. "I'm sorry. But I must be in the parade."

"Well, I tried," Cecelia laughed as she gave Fergus a push. "Be off with ye." She paused as he took her hands into his.

"Och. My macushla. My allana..." he reached across the small space between them and kissed her full on her red lips.

"Oh, Fergus. I love you..."

"Oh. Er. Ah, yes," George said softly as he and Sarah Jane looked to each other, astounded at the affection being shown between Fergus and Cecelia in only such a short time.

"We understand," Sarah Jane interrupted as the two separated and Fergus gave a short bow and departed. "Well, then," she continued as the three looked to each other. "One of our plans had been to find Susan's Dress Shop and here we are. Now we must find me some up-to-date clothing so that I can be the Belle of the Ball."

Oh, yes, Cecelia thought, now back to the present situation. The Belle of the Ball. Yes, that is why we are here, to find for my Sarah Jane the finest we can for the New Year's Ball at Fort Mackinac. Oh, yes. We must find her the best.

* * *

"Did you get enough sleep?" Marvin asked of Fred Ramsey as he joined the threesome of Captain Wilson, First Mate Davis and Fred in the pilot house a little after two o'clock in the hot and dry afternoon, not a breeze from the lake to cool them.

"I hope so. As much as I could with the unloading of the cargo next to my cabin. It wasn't easy," Fred responded, pleased that someone showed him some concern.

"And the same for me," Marvin agreed, seeing for the first time the young fellow not really as a reedy messenger but a young lad, now a promising lake sailor just like he was only two years ago when he first sailed on the *Centala*.

"Mr. Davis," Captain Wilson explained. "I called you here with the others as well as Mr. Beeman, who should be here shortly, to discuss our schedule here in Chicago and our return to Milwaukee. It seems we," he looked to Fred with a benign smile, "now have a new member to our pilot house crew. Not a messenger but a wheelsman apprentice."

Fred blushed as the first mate and Marvin each gave him a thumbs-up gesture with wide smiles in accepting him into their domain as it were.

"Ah. Here is Matt now," the captain continued as the second mate joined them. "Mr. Cole, I will have you and Mr. Beeman work together. You both do well together and are both experienced and I am sure will do us all well." He looked at Fred. "You will be with Mr. Davis." He gave the first mate a pretended stern look. "He can be quite demanding as you already know. But I know that you will learn much from him."

First Mate Davis gave Fred a smile and looked then to his captain with a friendly frown.

"So now then. We are paired, which is something. I have been concerned with this past time of being without a backup wheelsman since Bill Bailey left us for that tart in Milwaukee. I just hope he is happy. Mr. Davis, I would like you to set up a schedule of instruction in basic navigation and general seamanship for our Mr. Ramsey. He did very well on our run last night, even as tired as he was to begin with." He paused and looked to the chronometer. "The *Lady* is tied up until our departure at eleven this evening. We are now back on our schedule. Whatever your plans are I want us all back here by ten o'clock. Mr. Beeman and Mr. Cole will take the watch at eleven to be relieved by Mr. Davis and Mr. Ramsey at six in the morning for our entry into Milwaukee." The captain looked to the wharf below them. "Thank

God we had no problems with the unloading of the arms for the South." He gave a slight chortle. "The major was a little ticked with his men having to do most of the unloading of the arms. Oh, well, We are now rid of the arms..." He thought a moment. "The rifles for Captain Barry are safe and secure in the number three hold until tomorrow. Then we will have completed our task. Tasks, really. The delivery of the arms to the depot here in Chicago and the rifles for Barry's Union Guards. Oh," he realized that the foursome was still standing waiting for dismissal rather than his dialogue on the events they were all familiar with. "Ah, I'm sorry. You are dismissed. Enjoy your afternoon and evening. And... stay sober!"

CHAPTER ELEVEN

Friday, September 7, 1860

"What do you think happened to Bill?" Fred asked Marvin as they departed the gangway and proceeded across the Walchak Wharf for an afternoon and early evening in the big city.

"Oh, like others, he got himself tied up with a gal in a cathouse and said he was going to stay in Milwaukee to work and be near her."

"How old is he?" Fred asked as they turned onto Dearborn Street and headed in the direction of downtown Chicago.

"Old enough to know better," Marvin answered, stepping into the street to bypass a gathering on the sidewalk of a group of pan-handlers who were working on an elderly couple who, as Marvin guessed, made the mistake of offering a pittance to a hat-in-hand fellow. "I think he's about nineteen. He tried to act a lot older. Maybe that is why the cat in the whorehouse took up with him. He was a smooth talker."

"I never really got to know him too well. He kind of always ignored me."

"Yeah. Me too. I never really got to know him too well either. He was always at the cathouse in Milwaukee when we were in. But, believe it or not, he always stayed aboard in Houghton or Marquette and even in Mackinac."

"Weird."

"Well, now, me little bucko. What are your plans?" Marvin questioned as they approached the corner of Dearborn and Lake Streets.

"Well, I usually go to see a cousin of my mother's. A cousin of mine also," he added. "He has a printing business on Ninth Street, not far from here. He knows our schedule and has a lunch for me when the *Lady* gets in. He has three kids and I end up entertaining them until I have to get back to the boat at sailing time."

"But now? Today? Now that you are an honest-to-goodness apprentice wheelsman on one of the best boats on the lakes, what are your plans now?"

"Oh, I'll still see him and his wife and the kids. My mother would have a fit if I didn't see him when I was in Chicago and at least say hello... what are your plans?"

"Really nothing much. I like it better in Mackinac. I have some Indian friends and we usually go fishing or just goof around. As you know, we are in only long enough to pick up cargo and fuel, then we are off again. I'm usually back about supper time. I like the library at the post... they let me take books and some periodicals and return them when we get back. With our tight schedule it is only a week or two between my being in and out. So no big problem." He thought a moment. "I like the idea of the captain keeping the same schedule for us. I still have a full afternoon here with Matt. I'll get back early enough after supper for a nap and then will be ready to leave when he does."

"And me not until morning." Fred laughed at the thought of he with a full afternoon and evening until his need for duty at six in the morning.

"Fred, I want to be serious for a minute." Marvin took Fred by the arm and stood inside a store doorway. "Captain Wilson is one hell of a fine man. I know that Bill has disappointed him. But I don't want that to happen to you. The captain is giving you one big chance. Don't blow it. Do your best."

"Oh, Marv, I know. I'm only fifteen and... wow, here I am an apprentice on the *Lady Elgin*. I sure as hell will do my best to make the captain, and you, proud of me," a somewhat subdued Fred answered at his new friend's concern of his well-being.

"Ah. Listen," Marvin interrupted, not wanting to, but having no choice. "I hear a parade," he said as he turned to the sound of martial music coming down the street from the next block over. "Uh huh. I remember the captain meeting with an army lieutenant and some guys dressed in green militia uniforms from Milwaukee. Now I remember their talking of a parade they were to be in this afternoon. This must be it."

"A parade I haven't seen a parade in a long time. An Independence Day parade two years ago in Racine. Let's see this one now," an excited Fred said, finding something that could occupy his time for at least part of the afternoon other than playing with his young cousins. After all, he was now an apprentice wheelsman... a man!

* * *

"Captain Barry, Sir! Our men are all here but for Pat Cooney. I'm sure he will be with us when we get ready to push off," Fergus explained as the militia began assembling at Polk and LaSalle a little after twelve thirty.

"Good. Bring them together. We have a little time." The captain looked to his pocket watch. "We are supposed to start at one o'clock. But from the looks of things, it might be a little later." He took off his shako and wiped his sweating forehead with the back of his left hand. "This damn heat is beginning to take its toll of the party goers of last night," he added, looking to some forlorn figures slumped in the day's heat along the street sidewalks, recognizing many of them as the families of his militia men.

"Yes, it is getting quite muggy," Fergus agreed as he and others began to get into their positions. He was the point man for the second unit of the three divisions of Barry's Union Guards all joined together for the common good from the "Bloody Third Ward" on Milwaukee's south side to enjoy today's parade and some time spent in Chicago.

"We are to fall in behind the group from Whiting as they

106

pass. They seem to be a rag-tag group. Maybe they will make us look good," Captain Barry said proudly, now attired in his captain's uniform with its sash of gold and his dress sword at his waist, now all spit and polish. "My son and his friend will fall in behind our last unit. We are to be followed by a group of circus performers, doing w hat I don't know... maybe the boys will enjoy their antics."

"I see Pat is coming," Fergus offered. "At last count we are all here and raring to go."

"Have the drummers and fifers call to ready," Garret ordered, positioning himself in the lead of his militia. "Standard bearers," he again ordered, "to your positions and be ready. Sergeant O'Dell! Sergeant Kilbane! Sergeant Sweeny! Take your positions. Be ready to proceed on command."

The captain's orders, so well known and repeated over the two years since the founding of the Union Guards under his command, were immediately followed by the members as they took their positions and stood at parade rest awaiting the next order.

Captain Barry took a quick look at his pocket watch. One-twelve... not bad. He looked about the area now crowded with groups of other marching units preparing for their entries after his militia moved out. Bystanders and parade-goers, all in a high pitch of excitement, mingled about. Sounds from marching units already underway were now heard louder as the lead unit following an open wagon, pulled by a team of paired chestnut horses, in which were seated Stephen Douglas, the mayor of Chicago, and the grand marshal of the parade, all smiling and waving to the masses. The heat of the early afternoon was forgotten, only briefly, by the sight of 'The Little Giant,' a man who well might just be the next president, many thought, cheering him on.

The entourage proceeded past and moved on toward the city center, the street crowds being dispersed by constables and parade marshals with yellow derby hats. Three marching units passed with the flags of Peoria and Rockford, Illinois and Gary, Indiana, only fitfully, fluttering in the still mid-day air, now turning humid. A marching band from Northbrook was next, blaring and causing some viewers to cover their ears to the discordant sounds. Captain Barry then saw the group from Whiting following.

"AT...TENSHUN!" he commanded in a shrill voice used only on such occasions to carry over the din. The three units of Barry's Union Guards snapped to attention, the drummers and fifers at the ready. He then withdrew his sword from its sheath and pointed it towards the parade route as the Whiting group, now passing, gave him his signal to move out. "Forward... march! Column... left!" he commanded as the flag bearer of the first unit made its entrance into LaSalle Street to the beating of the drums and the trilling of the fifes.

Fergus, at his post, marked time then called "Forward" to his unit. "Column... left." Young Terrance Manning, the flag bearer, stumbled for only a moment, then caught himself and strode out to follow the proud and strutting first unit.

* * *

"Oh! I'm beat!" a near-exhausted Sarah Jane sighed as the three entered a wall booth of the saloon on the *Lady Elgin* after waiting for almost a half-hour to have a place to sit and rest.

"Och. And me too. My feet are killing me. But we did see some beautiful clothes. It was worth our try," Cecelia said as she slid in beside her mistress.

"Ah, my darling," George said, also feeling the drain of the day. "But it was worth it to see you as you will look at the cotillion on New Year's Eve. I don't know of any others at the fort who will have the opportunity as we have to come here to Chicago to do our shopping as we have. It has been a good time for us." He paused and wiped his brow with a napkin. "And yes, it has been a hot day. We'll wish we had a day like this come New Year's at the fort. Yet it was worth it. We have accomplished our bringing the arms for the depot and will have the arms for the militia in the morning. I think it has been worth our suffering," he stated as he looked about for a waiter and saw none available.

Cecelia took off her straw bonnet and pushed back a tress of her red hair. She half rose in her seat and looked out over the saloon toward the doors out onto the main deck.

"Looking for your man?" Sarah Jane asked with a knowing smile and nod.

"Yes. Oh yes. It is now just a little after three and we'd hoped the parade would have been over by now. So I do expect him any moment. It is lucky we have a place for him to sit and rest. I am sure his bum is about worn out from the marching and the heat of the day."

"Oh, I am sure that he will be along soon. I see some of the Green Yagers about and they were to have been marching behind Fergus's group," George offered as he contacted a hurrying waiter with a tray of empty water glasses. "Oh waiter.. well!" he laughed. "Well, what do you know? Mr. Rice! I see you are still a busy man and again as a waiter. Don't you ever rest?"

"Ah. Lieutenant Hartsuff. You can't believe how busy we have been today. The excursion of the militia groups from Milwaukee has been something else." The steward placed the tray on the table. "I've already made forty-eight cents in tips, and it's now just after three. And we still have the evening. I can't believe it! But I like it."

"Well, if you would like to make some more in tips, you can take our order." George motioned to the two women across from him. "We are all in need of refreshment."

"Let me get rid of these glasses and I'll be right back."

"Fine, but we expect a fourth. Ah! Here he is now," George said as he waved to Fergus who had entered the saloon and was looking for the three of them.

The steward picked up his tray and backed off as Fergus approached through the packed saloon.

Sarah Jane looked aside to Cecelia, who looked to the direction that George was motioning. Ah, Cecelia, she thought affectionately. The look in your eyes. I just cannot believe that what is happening is happening so fast. For these two years you have been with me, you never once let on once about a man. And there are many on the island. But now. Fergus, oh!

"Hello," a tired-looking but happy Fergus called with a short wave in return across the crowded aisleway. He slipped in beside George who moved to let him in beside him. He looked to Cecelia, who had a slight flush of her already tanned Irish face. "Hello my macushla," he almost whispered as they joined hands across the table.

"Hello my allana," Cecelia replied, also in almost a whisper. She gave him a wide smile as he leaned across and kissed her on the tip of her nose.

"Hey, you two." George nudged Fergus with a light touch of his elbow. "We have a little celebrating to do first."

"Oh, and what is it we are celebrating?" Fergus asked as he sat back but still held Cecelia's hands.

"First of all, Cecelia's birthday!"

"Oh!" Fergus raised his eyebrows as he looked at Cecelia. "You didn't say..."

"I was going to. We have so many other things to talk of."

"When?"

"Tomorrow."

"Then we really do have something to celebrate."

George continued, "Our being together. To having become friends. To having brought you and Cecelia together." George almost rambled, he, too, impressed and awed at the quick relationship between the two. "Oh," he then uttered as the steward returned and stood at the table with a wide smile.

"The drinks are on me," Fergus offered, looking to Cecelia, who nodded in agreement.

"No," the steward said, giving a slight bow. "It will be my pleasure to be the host on your first round. I had noticed the four of you last evening and a more complete foursome I have not seen for a long time. So. Please let me buy the first round." He backed up a step and stood tall for a short man.

"Well, then," Fergus granted, looking to the others. "If it's on you, you make the choice."

"Ah, Mr. Kilbane. Thank you. I know you will enjoy one of our new drinks, just recent to our offerings." He moved closer and leaned on the table edge. "It is a drink called a martinez and a lighter, more potent drink you will never have."

"A martinez..." George wondered at the sound. "It sounds... what? I don't know."

"Actually I don't know either. But it is very popular here in Chicago and I understand in many of the cities in the east. It is made of gin and vermouth. Some like it with a dash of lemon or a lemon slice. Others like it with a small pickled olive. All I know is that many like it." He stood back but was bumped so as to return to the table. "All I can say is, give it a try."

George looked to the others who each gave a shrug and a nod. "Four martinez," he asked with a flourish. "You make the choice of the garnish."

Fergus opened his neck band and gave a long sigh as the stewart departed. "Ah. my Cecelia," he said, again taking her hands in his. "To see you again..."

"Er. Ah." Sarah Jane interrupted. "I think we might want to change places." She offered a motion to George to allow Cecelia to be seated next to Fergus and she next to him.

"Now, then, Fergus," said George, "what are your plans? We are to be at the McVicar Theater by seven as the play begins at seven thirty. So we will have to have an early supper and just take scraps after the show on the *Lady*."

"I've checked and the time for our show of the Cyclorama and it starts at eight, Fergus answered. He looked to Cecelia. "Whatever you want to do I will go along with."

"Well, part of what we want to do is already answered by the waiter now coming with our order." She paused. "Mart... martinis," as she nodded to the approaching steward with a tray of four stemmed glasses and a large bowl of Saratoga chips.

* * *

"What you gonna do now?" Fred asked Marvin as the two picked their way through the now-scattering parade viewers on to other activities of the now-lengthening afternoon. Thunderclouds to the west and north were building with a portent of rain come evening, the warm, now moist air claiming the city streets.

"Oh, I don't know. It is a little too early to go back to the *Lady*. Sometimes I just walk about the docks and see what other boats are in and from where. I like to hear others tell of their time on the lakes. They can be really scary at times." The two stood at the street corner of LaSalle and Madison Streets. "What about you? Are you going to see your cousins?"

"Oh, I don't know. One is a real crybaby. My Aunt Laura is really nice but can get grouchy." Fred thought a moment. "Yeah, I suppose I should. It's not too far and I can tell them I have to be back to the boat early as I am now an apprentice wheelsman. And... yeah! You can come with me. We'll stay only a little while then still be able to be together until we do have to be back."

"Well, I really do want to get back early. Matt and I have the run tonight and I should get a little rest if I can. But I guess we could find something else to do after we see them," Marvin agreed, thankful that he now had someone to share his time ashore. And he really liked the skinny guy.

The two headed south on LaSalle. "Where you from?" Fred asked, his curiosity now aroused because of their new friendship.

"Oh, a little town in northern Michigan. Alpena."

"Alpena? Never heard of it."

"It's a lumbering and fishing town. My folks came from Port Huron three years ago. My pa is a barrel maker and was needed by a company for shipping fish. So they came up with me and my two sisters."

"How'd you get on the *Lady Elgin*?"

112

"Well, I wasn't too happy with the winter and my folks knew it, so one day when a lumber schooner pulled in, I found they needed a hand, so I came aboard. I was just sixteen, three years ago. Later that summer I went aboard another boat out of Muskegon, where I was asked to be an apprentice wheelsman. I got my papers last summer, and so here I am now, on the *Lady Elgin* where I hope to stay for a long time."

Fred frowned. "I'm from Kenosha, and in the winter the boats don't sail either." He thought a second. "What do you do in the winter?"

"Well, the first winter the *Susie Q*, that was its name, tied up in Mackinac. And it was worse than if it had tied up in Alpena. But my second winter, two years ago, I went south. I was on the *Centala* that tied up here in Chicago with three others and sailed on the riverboats out of Paducah, Kentucky."

"But it snows there, too," Fred wondered, not too sure.

"Oh yeah. But the river doesn't freeze over like the rivers or shorelines do up here."

"Oh. I see."

Marvin continued, pleased that Fred was interested in his background, and giving him a chance to brag a bit. "I sailed on the stern-wheeler *Blue Bird*, a rear paddle wheeler. Not like our side paddle ones. As a crewman."

"Yeah, I've seen pictures of them."

"Last winter I sailed again out of Paducah but on the *Biloxi Belle* and because I had my papers as a First Class Wheelsman from last summer, I was able to sail as an assistant pilot, as they are called on the river, not as an apprentice, or cub as they are also called. I hope that I can again work with a great guy, Sam Clemens, a guy funny as hell and a damn good river pilot. He can teach me a lot."

"Do you suppose I could go with you this winter?" a now truly excited Fred asked.

"I don't know," a now serious Marvin cautioned. "You're only fifteen. Really young to be an apprentice at all. You're a real cub."

"You were sixteen," Fred noted, a touch petulant.

"Yes. But I am taller and heavier than you. I don't think anyone ever questioned my age. And," he continued, "the work as a crewman is damn hard. You would need more meat on your bones. If I didn't have my First Class papers I don't think I would have gone back. As it is I have to still learn a lot of the difference between a lake sidewheel steamer's helm than a river steamer with its stern-wheel. A hell of a difference." Marvin paused, seeing a more contemplative Fred now seeming to understand. "And besides. It is a different world down there along the rivers and their ports. We see only the bigger ports... here in Chicago... Milwaukee... Houghton...even Mackinac. On the Mississippi and Ohio, there are a few big cities, but we have to stop at almost every little town. On the *Lady* we burn coal, on the boats on the river they mostly use wood. A lot of wood. So they make more stops. And besides, when we are in a city or town for any time the first place to go is a..." he paused again..."a whorehouse. Some have two or three."

"A whorehouse. A cathouse."

"Yeah. Most of the men are married and away from their homes for the season. Really all year, if they sail north in the summer and south in the winter."

"Wow!" Fred exclaimed. "Eh... have you ever..."

"Only once. In Memphis," Marvin replied, almost apologetically.

Fred took a new tack. "Do you have a girlfriend?"

Marvin smiled and shook his head. "No. Not really. But I do see a girl when I'm in Houghton. I feel I have too much to learn about being a First Class Wheelsman first. Later I'll think about a wife and having children. I've got plenty of time. The girl I see, Thelma Hinks, is caring for an ailing mother and doesn't want to make any plans for herself for awhile. But, hey," he interrupted himself, "I'm getting hungry. The *Lady* is closed down until ten so we should get something now. What about you?"

114

* * *

"Hey! Hey there fellows." A voice called from behind them. Fred and Marvin turned to the call and saw a young dapper fellow in a tan jacket, a dark brown derby with long tan pants topping patent leather oxfords. He approached them with a wide smile. "Hi! I'm Jamie and I just saw the two of you and you both look like you just might enjoy some female company for the evening."

"Oh?" Marvin questioned, having met this type before in other locales. He stood bold, knowing a pimp when he saw one.

"Ah. Hold it my friend," the fellow said, holding his hands up, realizing Marvin's reaction. "I'm just trying to help you. Both of you..." he eyed Fred. wondering of his age, "to a fine evening of entertainment. Here," he offered a card. "In the event you are looking for a form of pleasant fun. You might be interested in this establishment which provides a fine evening of dancing and other niceties with very pleasant young ladies." He winked knowingly.

Marvin took the card, realizing what was meant.

"Have a good evening," the pimp nodded as he sidled off, seeking other prospects in the milling streets.

"What?" Fred questioned, this being his first encounter with the type and not too sure what it was all about, judging from Marvin's reaction.

"Oh, you see his kind everywhere." Marvin gave a snide smile. "He's called a pimp. This card is for..." he read from it, "Enjoy an evening of pleasure to the music and dancing provided by the 'Darling Dancing and Singing Club' at 458 1/2 North Water Street, Upstairs. Hmm, only a few blocks from here. It's supposed to be a dancing parlor but it's really a whorehouse... a house of ill repute," he added.

"Marvin?" Fred posed.

"Eh." Sensing.

"Could we try it?"

115

"My God! You're only fifteen!"

"At least let's see what it's like. It sounds like fun. I'm excited!"

"Oh boy." Marvin puffed his cheeks. "So am I. But let's get supper first. I'm starving!"

* * *

"George." You're back early." Captain Wilson greeted his first mate as he struck a loco-foco to his pipe, a somber look on his face.

"Oh, I've got some things to do and it's too damn hot and now getting muggy to walk the streets," George Davis commented as he entered the pilot house a little after five o'clock, surprised at his captain being there.

"Aye. I feel the same. I was able to take care of our business with Voight, our head bookkeeper sooner than I thought, and the Port Authority too, so I went up to the Merchant's Hotel to see if anyone was around to have a drink with. But it was too crowded, and as you said, too damned hot to walk the streets. So I thought I'd check the loading and also check for the run tonight to Milwaukee, and hope that all our passengers will be back on time for us to leave at eleven."

"Just how many did we take aboard in Milwaukee?" an equally concerned first mate asked as he tapped his pipe.

"Stephan says 348 according to his ticket count, but he thinks we have more than that. Many more."

"From the way they packed our decks I would think so," George agreed.

The two stood quietly for a minute or two, both scanning the waterfront area. The Port of Chicago this late Friday afternoon was active with boats of all shapes and sizes plying the river. "Oh ho. There is the *Megan*. I haven't seen her since she went ashore near Toledo three years ago. I didn't know she was still sailing," George commented as a propeller steamed towards

116

the open waters of Lake Michigan, its bow wave action causing the *Lady* to have a slight rise and fall.

"George," the captain said as he exhaled a long drag from his pipe.

"Yes, Jack," George answered at his captain's serious tone, coupled with his somber mood he noted when he came in, their using first names only when together alone.

"One thing I did do today, after I met with Voight and maybe the real reason for not really wanting a drink with friends but rather to get back here..." Jack paused and drew on his pipe.

"And that was?"

"This is my last trip. From here to Milwaukee."

"What!" a stunned first mate gasped.

"Yes." Jack turned and looked to his first mate and friend for these past two seasons.

"After my to-do with Voight this afternoon, I began to realize that here we are almost into the fall and I haven't seen my Elaine or the children since..." he paused again and looked away with a choke in his voice. "I sometimes wonder if they even realize they have a father."

"But... I... I'm sure Elaine understands," a still-surprised George hoped.

"Oh, hell yes. She knows the need for the money. But she also must know that the children, especially Hazel with her condition, needs a full-time father." He took another draw. "I have the farm. Elaine's brother Alfred is taking care of it as well as one of his own. I'm sure it must be most difficult for him and his family. But today with Voight... Mr. Andrew Voight," Jack said disparagingly, "I think that clinched some thoughts I have had for the past few weeks. Months, really."

"Oh? How?" a perplexed George asked as he drew on his pipe.

"Well, as usual the Hubbard bookkeeping department, Mr. Voight, Head Honcho, is quite demanding of our records. This Voight is something else. He and I had a run-in a few years ago, before you came aboard..."

George nodded, having heard rumors.

"and has never let me forget it. I screwed up in okaying an inventory that was set up by the clerk at the time that was way out of line. The bastard was hustling and cost us money. But I took responsibility for it and Voight has never let me forget about it."

"Hell, Jack, I've been with you these past two seasons and would never question your capabilities."

"Ah, maybe not as a boat captain but I did, and I do, rely on my clerk's abilities. Our clerk now, Stephan, I trust with my life. But then Mr. Moneybags has let it fester and would you believe he brought it up again this afternoon. That's when I said 'Bullshit!' I'm done."

"Jack!" George almost pleaded, now understanding of his captain's concern. "Hell. Your home is in southern Michigan closer to Detroit than from here in Chicago. Stay with us until at least back to Mackinac. Damn it all. I want you to stay until the season is over."

The captain turned to his first mate again and bit his lower lip. He thought a moment and drew again on his pipe. "Maybe you're right." He gave a weak smile. "Maybe I'm too steamed up to think straight. And yes," he added, "I could give you time to think about taking over from me rather than my dropping it on you tomorrow morning without any warning. I'm glad we have had this talk. It should give you some thoughts as to what you will want to do. I would hope you would be promoted to the *Lady*'s captain... ah... yes... I can wait until Mackinac."

George took a long pull on his pipe and slowly shook his head at the thought of his being the captain of the *Lady Elgin*. "Oh my God."

CHAPTER TWELVE

Friday, September 7, 1860

"And how did ye enjoy your visit back to the 'auld sod?'" Pat Cooney asked of Fergus and Cecelia as they were heading out through the side door of Kingsbury Hall facing Clark Street, along with others who had enjoyed the trip many of them would have never recognized as being like the one they remembered in the days of the "Great Hunger" as the famine of the forties was now called.

"Och. It was grand," Fergus answered in a lilting sort of way he picked up from the program, having lost most of his Irish lingo over the years as he and Cecelia walked close together. "I am amazed at how it was done. A true miracle of modern ingenuity. Although they call it a cyclorama, I would call it a panorama as it rolled out from the two pillars supporting the scenes in front of us. But no mind, I found it entertaining."

"Yes. I, too was impressed," Pat agreed. "It is quite an under-taking and the pictures were that true, as best I can recall."

Fergus nodded in agreement. "I especially enjoyed the scenes along the Galway Coast and the Aran Islands. I visited them as a lad with an uncle and was, as you were with the program, impressed. And this panorama has brought back some remem-brances. The islands are the only true Ireland left."

"And I enjoyed the singing," Cecelia added. "That young fellow... Michael MacCoy, is such a beautiful tenor and his sister on the harp. Ah, grand. It brought back memories."

"Yes. I noticed your wiping your eyes a number of times, as

did I." Fergus smiled to her, his appreciating her sense of feeling for her... his and the others their youth... now years gone by.

"I was at first... ah..." Pat searched for a word, "ah, skeptical. My days as a lad showed me many a different scene of the landscape. What I remembered is the people dying in the famine. He shrugged at the remembrance. Yet the program does bring back memories of the beauty of the land I'd almost forgotten. Aye. I am glad we came to see it rather than go to something else. I only wish my little one John was able to see it, but he fell asleep through most of it."

"Och. He and Nora are too young to ever know. She watched and seemed interested, but they both need sleep. Och. Yes, so do I," Molly Cooney said in her deep Killarney brogue.

"But look at 'em now," Pat chuckled as the two went darting in and out of the sidewalk crowd, playing tag.

The group made its way with others out into the evening with the skies now in deep clouds, the humidity high. "I wonder how George and Sarah Jane have enjoyed their seeing that Mary McVicar," Cecelia said as the two moved along with the crowd. "From what I have read in the Tribune, she is supposed to be quite an actress."

"Yes, and I hope George enjoyed it. He seemed to be quite a little tipsy when they left us after supper," Fergus remembered.

"Och. I think we were all a little tipsy. I know I really felt the three ones that I had, those... martinez... they tasted different but... it's not like brandy or a good whiskey. I... it kinds of sneaks up on one," Cecelia admitted. "But! I am hungry, our not really eating a supper, of only the potatoes and the dinner salad. Och! I am starving."

"Yes. And I, too am starving. We're almost to the wharf," Fergus stated as he saw a large number of the militia units gathering into their own groups, preparing for the return to the *Lady*.

"With this number of people will we be able to get aboard in time for our leaving?" Pat wondered.

"We were told not to be later than ten o'clock," Fergus replied as he saw Garret making his way toward them with his son and friend in tow. "And how was your banquet?" he asked as the crowd began a mass movement toward the loading ramp now being lowered to bring them aboard. He looked to the gangway which was roped off, knowing that the First Class passengers were also getting ready to board, but in a more orderly fashion.

"It went well. Senator Douglas is one hell of an orator," Garret answered, glad to see his friend after a hectic day and evening. "He is truly sincere and concerned about our future as a nation these next few months. We can only pray to God that cool heads will prevail in both the North and the South from those who want secession... from either side."

"I still would like to know what Rufus King was doing in Milwaukee on the ready, as it were, with his militia. They looked mean as hell," Fergus wondered as the milling crowd began boarding amid a now calming and wearisome throng, the day almost now over and a six- or seven-hour run yet to Milwaukee.

"What do you think of the weather?" Pat, now carrying his son who was again now sleeping, but fitfully, asked Garret.

"It seems to be building. It has cooled a bit with the coming of the night and I see the lamps flickering, which means a breeze is about. Maybe by the time we leave whatever weather is holding will have passed us by."

"The captain knew what to do coming down from the Beaver Island storm and the delay he had," Fergus added. "I am sure he will sail only if it is the safe thing to do."

Cecelia, now almost exhausted from the long day and the events of the entire past two days, panted as the steep ramp made walking difficult. Fergus put his arm around her waist and helped her along. Throughout the day and until even now, she had been thinking of what the night and early tomorrow would bring her in her thinking of her relationship with Fergus. Oh, no question that she loved him. Och. What a man. She would marry him in a minute if he were to ask. But... she does have a responsibility to Sarah Jane and she does have her clothing and personal items in Mackinac. Not much, but it is all that I have... and the *Lady* would be on its return trip south in a week... two weeks... whatever. Yes. That is what I will do, she finally decided... I will return with Sarah Jane to Mackinac for my things as well as to help her in needing a new maid. And it will give Fergus time to let his friends and employees know of his plans to be married. Yes. He can make the plans for us to be married in his parish church, St. John's, soon to become a cathedral. Och. That would be grand... yes. I will tell them... Fergus, Sarah Jane and George, just as soon as we get together.

* * *

"How do you feel?"

"Oh, I've felt better. Those martinez drinks are something else. They got to me."

"Yeah. And to me, too. But we did have a good time. That Fergus is quite a comedian for a mortician," George laughed. "It was lucky we were able to get back to our cabin and have a rest before going to the theater. As it was I slept through most of it. I don't know of from a hangover or the play itself. It kind of dragged."

"I know. I had to nudge you a few times when you started to snore. It did seem a little melodramatic and slow. That Mary McVicar is a good actress, although at her age of her mid-thirties or early forties, playing a teenage girl. Eh."

"I wonder how Fergus and Cecelia enjoyed their program," George commented as they exited the theater and joined with others on the crowded sidewalks and made their way down Lake Street to the *Lady*.

"Oh, I am sure they did. From what I read of it in the paper, it is quite a unique production. I almost wish now that we had made plans to have seen it with them."

"Well, we can tell each other of our evening and maybe feel we shared each other's entertainment. Ah, there is the *Lady*

122

Elgin," George exclaimed, at the Walchak Wharf which was now covered with returning exhausted but happy and fulfilled excursionists boarding by way of the loading ramp.

"At least we don't have to be in the crowd," Sarah Jane commented with a motion to the First Class gangway that they were approaching with only a minimum of passengers ascending. "It's too bad that Cecelia isn't with us. It must be hectic for her in that crowd."

"Ah, but you must remember that she is with Fergus," George allowed with a grin. "She's probably walking on air."

* * *

"Well now. What do we have here?" A middle-aged woman with jet black hair, in a dark blue dress tight to her voluptuous body and holding a glass of whiskey in her right hand and a cigarette in her left, greeted Marvin and Fred as they entered the main room of an upstairs apartment from a steep stairway. There was a small dance floor which had four doorways facing on to it, three with hanging rope portiers covering closed doors while the other was paneled with two red glass panes.

Fred tried to look wordly as Marvin had coached him to act, but his searching eyes looked about the room in awe. Marvin looked aside to Fred and wondered what in the hell ever let him bring Freddy to such a place as this. I must be out of my mind, he thought. "We were told by a..." he began, "a young fellow that there was dancing here..."

"Oh, yes. We have dancing here. And we also sell spirits," the woman agreed. "But we do like our ladies to dance with a little older man." She motioned with her glass to Fred. "I'm sorry, as much as I would like to, he is too young." She sized up Marvin with a wink of her left eye. "You. You. We can have you enjoy one of our girls as she entertains you with dancing... or whatever."

Fred, so taken by the fact he was in a whorehouse, looked around the room seeing that it had heavily-draped windows with

123

sofas and divans on which were seated or lounging, a number of young to middle-aged couples in various degrees of excitement and wanting. In one corner was an upright piano with no sheet music on its rack. In the center of the room was a small, what he guessed, was the dance floor, a space of about six by six as best he could figure. Awful small for a dance floor, he thought, remembering some back home in Kenosha, especially with the number of people in the room. He counted nine, including the woman now sipping her drink, with a smile to Marvin over its rim. He didn't know how many were in the rooms beyond.

Marvin realized that Fred was too young to have been brought to this place. He had made a big mistake and decided they should leave now. Pronto. "Oh, no. We were just wondering and wanted to see what it was really like. We had hoped to do some dancing. But we understand," he said as he took Fred by his left arm and the two headed back down the steep stairway, Fred somewhat reluctantly.

"Hey. I understand. Come back when you're ready!" the woman called, laughing as the two fled.

"Wow! What a place!" Fred almost exploded "I've been to a whorehouse... a cathouse," as they reached the sidewalk and headed back toward the city center and the *Lady*.

"Yeah. It was quite a place. I wondered about your age. You do look pretty young. I'm glad she wouldn't take care of us. Hey. Maybe next time... what's that?" They turned to the sound of neighing horses to see a Chicago police paddy wagon pulling up to the front of the house with a band of policemen armed with billy-clubs charging up the stairway.

"Yeah," Fred agreed, understanding that something big was going on and that they left in the nick of time to avoid being caught with the others. And he having not done anything.

The two turned again to the *Lady*, now at a leisurely pace, each wondering what might have been but not wanting to tell anyone of their experience in a Chicago whorehouse.

* * *

The oompah beats of a tuba player dressed in the uniform of a Black Yager along with a fifer and a fiddler trilling discordant passages of familiar marches and popular songs carried out from the saloon to the gangway. "My God. Some of them are still playing songs and even dancing," Sarah Jane commented as she and George checked in with Chief Steward Rice and looked to the saloon where any number of assorted militia men and their waives or sweethearts still frolicked, along with any number of children.

"Oh. Something like this only happens once or twice every couple of years to these people," George commented. "They feel they deserve a break and are now really taking advantage of the situation. They'll pay for it the next few days. But for now? Hey! Live it up."

"Yes. I suppose so," Sarah Jane agreed, amazed at the enthusiasm shown by the now rollicking group about a young fellow in the uniform of a Green Yager, playing spoons on his knees in the manner of a member of the Black Combo they had all seen earlier.

"Good evening Lieutenant Hartsuff," Chief Steward Rice greeted them. "I trust you had a full day of excitement. I understand the parade, with the various militia we transported, was a great success and that the oration of Senator Douglas was exceptional."

George nodded and presented his ticket stub as a bona fide passenger on a return trip to Milwaukee with his wife and her maid. "You have quite a crowd in the deck passengers. And I also see that you have a large number of First Class passengers coming aboard as well," he commented, wondering of the number and what the *Lady* could handle.

"Oh, we have had more. This is a large group and I am sure we will handle them with no problem. What I am impressed with, though, on this trip is who we now have aboard." He paused and leaned to Sarah Jane. "Here, take a look at my list."

He pointed to a listing of First Class passengers now boarding. "Here, look. Would you believe we have a member of the British Parliament... the Honorable Herbert Ingram and a son. And look again. Colonel Francis Lumsden, a co-owner of the New Orleans Picayune, one of the most prestigious newspapers in the South, and his wife and son and daughter. And you wondered why I knew your name. Ah, Lieutenant. With names like these on a roster, it pays to know who is who."

"Well, the *Lady Elgin* does have a fine reputation, both the captain and the vessel. I am sure that word and print has gotten over the years..." George said as he and Sarah Jane moved on to allow those following to come aboard.

"I do hope we will be able to see Cecelia and Fergus," Sarah Jane said as she scanned the passengers. "I would like to freshen up and I am sure she would also. They should be back by now."

"Oh, I'm sure they are. Everyone was told to be back no later than ten o'clock. He pointed to the loading ramp now almost empty of stragglers, most deck passengers now aboard.

"Well, I would like to get to my cabin. I've got to pee..." Sarah Jane frowned.

"And I should check the rifles... er, the Indian artifacts and..." George pretended a slip.

"Oh. I know." Sarah Jane gave him a shush with her right hand. "I must hurry. See if you can find Cecelia and Fergus."

* * *

"What do you make of the weather, Mr. Davis?"

"I don't know. First Mate Davis looked to the barometer. "The pressure is holding and the wind has kicked up a bit. But the buildup seems to be heading more to the east," he answered to his captain as he entered the pilot house now in the glow of the compass lamps, an uneasy darkness now having settled over the riverfront of Chicago.

In attendance with Captain Wilson was Second Mate Matt Beeman, Wheelsman Marvin Cole, Ship's Clerk Stephan Caryl and the Chief Steward Fred Rice. "I've waited purposely to see just what way the wind was blowing, as the saying goes," the captain stated. "I want to get your opinions on our moving out. We are now almost a half hour late and Mr. Caryl here says that any number of the First Class passengers, along with some of the deck passengers, are getting a little testy and want us on our way."

"Oh, hell yes. I'm sure they could be. Many of the deck passengers are spent and worn out, and I am sure have to be back to work tomorrow and would like a good night's rest," the first mate reasoned.

"And there are still those who are continuing their excursion," the chief steward added, happy with the money being brought in, but not with the effort needed.

"We also have many more aboard now than when we left Milwaukee," the clerk also informed the group, the chief steward nodding in agreement.

"Well, we'll just have to make up our minds as to what we will have to do. We can lay over for the night, but that will screw up our schedule to Milwaukee and Mackinac as we all know, and the connections of some of our First Class passengers to other lines," the captain stated as he tamped tobacco into his pipe. "Mr. Cole, do you have any suggestions?"

Marvin looked to the darkened sky above the harbor, low clouds reflecting the lights of the Walchak Wharf.

"Well," he pondered, pleased to have been asked for his contribution to the general concern, "the wind seems to have picked up a bit," he nodded, agreeing with the first mate's comment. "The weather could well be mostly past us. It has been a long day and most weather such as this, as best I understand it, has moved on to the east."

Captain Wilson lit his pipe and contemplated for a few moments.

"Mr. Rice, get the word out that the *Lady* is sailing." He looked to the chronometer. "It is now twelve after eleven. We will depart at eleven-thirty. Get the crew and circulate among the passengers that we will be leaving in only minutes."

"What of those who don't want to leave? They seem to be having a hell of a good time," the clerk stated, knowing of the festivities still going on.

"They can get a free ride to Milwaukee but sure as hell will have to pay for the return trip back to Chicago," Captain Wilson said sarcastically. "Mr. Beeman, prepare to get underway. Notify the engine room to stand by. Mr. Davis, see that the cattle are damn well secured in the event of foul weather. I want them all tethered. Ah, Mr. Ramsey," he greeted Fred as he entered the pilot house. "I am glad that you are here. I might need a messenger after all until we get underway and out into open waters."

"Yes, Sir," Fred responded as he stepped into the pilot house and moved aside as the first mate, the chief steward and the clerk all took their leave in going about their business of getting the *Lady* ready to get underway.

"Hi," he said to Marvin who was studying the charts of the river and its exit into Lake Michigan. "I thought I'd come and see what you were doing and say good night..." He paused. "But now?"

"As you know, Mr. Ramsey, it can get a little busy now on the bridge the next hour or so. The experience will do you good," said Captain Wilson. He paused. "In fact...messenger...Fred...Mr. Ramsey," the captain corrected, "I'll put you to work right now. Tell Mr. Rice that I want the bar shut down just as soon as possible. If we do encounter any bad weather...I was not happy with it's being open during the bad weather at Beaver Island." He drew on his pipe. "I know it will be hard, but I want it done."

"Yes, Sir," Fred answered as he gave a short wave to Marvin and left with a smile to his newfound friend and fellow wheelsman.

* * *

"Ah, Fergus," George called, surprised to find Fergus and Garret Barry with three other militia men in the compartment where the rifles were stored.

"George," Fergus replied, also surprised. "We thought we had better check out the rifles. They seem to be in good shape, thanks to you."

"Yes," Garret added as he joined the two. "Your quick action this morning, I've been told by Fergus, could well have prevented us from getting the rifles. I can understand the major accepting the other arms, if he had learned somehow that our boxes were really rifles." He paused. "Who knows what he might have done? So thank you again," he said as he extended his right hand.

"Thank you, sir," George answered, pleased that he was of such help to the captain and his cause.

"Now then," Fergus said as the group left the compartment. "Cecelia left me to go to your wife and tidy up. I must say the day has taken its toll on her... and me," he added, wiping his brow, the two now walking together.

"Oh, yes. On all of us. We still have some time before we sail and I've got to find a place to spend the night, and Sarah Jane wants us to get together again and celebrate Cecelia's birthday tomorrow. Maybe we can have a little touch of something..." George hinted.

"No martinez!" Fergus raised his hands as if to fend off "They were good. They were different... but they were potent. I felt them all evening."

"And I too," George laughed.

Fergus, now serious, said, "Cecelia too wants us to get together. She wants to make up her mind just what she must do. We must make our plans. I truly love her. I have waited many a year for just the such as her. A truly beautiful woman." He smiled. "She is Irish... she is Catholic... she wants children. And I also am the same."

The two stopped at the base of the stairway leading from the main deck to the hurricane deck to allow the passing of a group of Black Yagers. "Oh, ho, yes. It is obvious. It is really something from heaven the way you two have met. And Sarah Jane and I both feel responsible for it."

"Yes," Fergus said, again serious. "And it because of our mutual concern for the future of our nation that brought the four of us together. Your Captain Pratt and my Captain Barry, both men of the same cloth... as it were... are way far and ahead of many who hardly seem to be aware of our future."

"Well, many who are not concerned now will surely be within the next two months. Things are coming to a head and only God knows what the future will bring come the first of the year."

* * *

"Och. I think I was doing fine until we had to climb up the steep ramp, it being so warm and muggy," Cecelia said wearily as she unhooked her corset lace and gave a sigh of relief.

"Yes. Even the steep gangway steps were something," Sarah Jane added as she touched a comb to her hair. "I feel much better now that I've changed. It has been a wonderful trip, even with the storm coming down from Mackinac, but I will be glad getting back to more familiar surroundings."

"Miss Sarah..." Cecelia said softly and with a little hesitation.

"Yes," Sarah Jane answered, not sure for Cecelia's hesitancy.

"Miss Sarah, Fergus and I had a long talk. He has asked me to marry him."

"Why, that's wonderful! I said only last night how happy I am for you! But do you have a problem?"

Cecelia gave a shy smile. "No... er... no. Not really. I just feel that I should return to Mackinac with you. First to get my things, not much but all I have, and also to help you in getting another girl. Corine Riley I know would love to be with you. Or maybe the Indian girl Namid."

"Oh, thank you. I know I will need a little time to get used to someone else. We have been together these past two wonderful years. I honestly feel you are the sister I never had. What did Fergus think of your thoughts?"

"Oh, I told him I wanted to talk to you first. I do not want to leave you so suddenly."

"Oh, Cecelia you are so wonderful to me. I am sure if you left us abruptly in Milwaukee, I might have been hurt and disappointed. Now we can be together a little while longer. And do you know what? We might even come back with you for the wedding."

"Oh, Sarah," Cecelia gushed as the two clasped and held each other. "Today I am the happiest woman in the world!"

* * *

"Mr. Beeman, signal for the stern hawsers to be slipped," Captain Wilson commanded as he stepped aside the wheelsman, Marvin Cole. He looked to the chronometer. "Eleven thirty-three," he noted.

The second mate gave the pull bell that alerted the deck gang aft to signal the wharf dockmen to cast off the hawser of the *Lady*. "Stand by, Mr. Cole," the captain added as he nodded to the second mate to pull for the engine room to commence to slow reverse. "Have the bow hawsers slipped," he said as the side wheels began churning slowly astern with a rumbling of waters filling the air. The *Lady* backed from the Walchak Dock, the lookouts posted and looking for movements on the dark waters, seeing only small craft, not enough to be worried about.

The *Lady* gained maneuvering room in mid-river and began a slow turn as the second mate pulled for an "ahead slow" toward the river's entry into Chicago Harbor and points east into Lake Michigan. "Put her at due east... ninety degrees," the captain ordered. "We'll keep at that heading until we are sure we have a straight run to Milwaukee. It should be in about another hour and a half," he added.

The *Lady Elgin* moved through the late night darkness into light seas from the northwest. She met the movement with slow rolling from beam to beam, taking the motions in her stride. "We will continue at ninety degrees... due east at twelve knots for the next hour and a half," the captain stated as he lit his pipe and blew a thick cloud of smoke to the ceiling. "Mr. Davis, you might want to take to your quarters for some rest. Six o'clock can come mighty early. I'm not too sure of our weather through the night and I do want you if I need you."

The captain drew another drag. "Mr. Ramsey. You did fine this morning and I am proud of you. I also want you to be ready for your turn at six. It is now almost midnight so you too will want to get a good night's rest." He took another drag. "It has been a long haul for all of us these past two days," he added as he gave a yawn. "What is your guess on the weather. Mr. Beeman?"

"The winds are steady from the northwest, not too heavy, but carrying discomfort for some, I'm sure."

"Mr. Cole?"

"We are holding fine. No problems, just a slight drift that can be corrected."

"Well then, we are now on our way to Milwaukee. Let us hope that the storm potential is less as we are now out on the open waters," Captain Wilson said, now showing signs of his own susceptibility to the demands of being a captain. "I believe the storm threat is now behind us and to the south." He stifled another yawn. "Mr. Beeman, I believe I'll take a nap. It has been a long day," he looked to his staff, "for all of us. Mr. Beeman, you will call me if anything comes up, of course."

"Of course, Sir."

"Now then, I bid you adieu. The *Lady* is now in your good hands." The captain then turned and entered the door to his private room off the rear of the pilot house. He gave a sigh as he took off his coat and pulled at his tie. Oh, I'm tired, so tired, he thought as he stretched out on his bed, fully clothed. His leaving the *Lady* in Mackinac. Is it the right thing to do? This past year has taken so much for me. I just don't know how much more I can take. Elaine... the children... Voight... the storm the other day... the weather tonight. Hell, I should have stayed over but as Voight said, we must maintain our schedules. The company's reputation depends on our doing so. He gave a brief chuckle... so!

The motion of the *Lady* was lulling as he lay trying to contemplate his future. I am now forty years old, soon to be forty-one, and getting on in years. I have never regretted my going on the water as a lad, for a few years I thought, then get a farm. Ah, that I have done, but I am still sailing with a farm. A sudden rise in one of the swells caused him a moment of concern. Oh, hell. Let Matt worry about what might be, he's all set to...

"Captain! Captain Wilson! Come quick!" He heard Matt's voice and a pounding on the door.

CHAPTER THIRTEEN

Saturday, September 8, 1860

"Happy birthday to you. Happy birthday to you. Happy birthday, dear Cecelia. Happy birthday to you'" the threesome of Fergus, Sarah Jane and George sang gaily to Cecelia as they held their whiskey glasses high in a toast at one minute after midnight.

"Och. You are such silly ones." She blushed at their enthusiasm.

"And would you believe I don't know how old you are?" Fergus stated as he took a sip.

"Never you mind. You'll find out soon enough on our wedding license application," she laughed, taking a sip from her glass.

The foursome, now close friends, gathered in the First Class cabin of Sarah Jane and Cecelia. Most of the discussion of the late evening and early morning hours of Saturday, September 8, 1860 was for the plans of Cecelia and Fergus to be married in the fortnight at St. John's Cathedral in Milwaukee.

"Sarah Jane said earlier that maybe we might be able to attend your wedding," George stated, "But you must remember I am in the army and here with you now by orders from my commanding officer, Captain Pratt." He raised his glass in a toast, the others raising theirs in accord. "Well, I know I am bushed," he added, "and would like a little sleep. We'll be well on our way to Mackinac again tomorrow and I hope I can find time to get some time to rest. The army's demands don't excuse Sundays and I know I have the duty on Monday. So then, what are our plans for the rest of the night?"

"Why not stay here in our cabin?" Sarah Jane offered, looking to Cecelia. "Oh, not that way!" she laughed at Cecelia's look on her face with a "What!" expression. She giggled. "You and I can sleep together in our bed. The men can sleep on the floor. It's the best we can do. And we even have our own commode, so we don't have to run to the public toilet."

"As adults I guess we can behave ourselves," Fergus laughed at the situation and Cecelia's reaction. "I guess I can wait."

Cecelia covered her mouth of just taking a swallow and almost spewing it out in a burst of laughter.

"Oh. Yes," Fergus said, now realizing the late hour. Or was it the early hour? he wondered. "It is late and I do believe we should all try to get some sleep." He finished his last dreg. "I must be at my mortuary today at eight o'clock. And I still have to spend a full day. Death knows no time limits." He looked to his watch. "It is now almost two o'clock and I can tell by the roll of the boat it might not be the smoothest night we will have. I just hope I will be asleep in only a few minutes. So please, let's make our final good nights and all hit the hay."

* * *

"Aye, George. I can see!" Captain Wilson called as he entered the pilot house on the run, now seeing the approaching squall line bearing down on the *Lady* from the northwest with lightning flashes illuminating and thunder crackling sounding along the horizon. He shouted to Marvin over the din of now-crashing rain on the windows. "What are you heading?"

A now-struggling wheelsman shouted back, "Ninety-four degrees and moving up," as the full force of the squall broadsided the *Lady*, causing her to lean precipitously to starboard with the frothing waters now upon her.

"Head her in!" Captain Wilson almost screamed. "Meet it head on! Matt! Get with him." He pointed to Marvin who was now struggling to hold the helm. He then pulled the bell pull cord for increase in speed as the *Lady* with great effort by its wheelsmen began a laborious turn left to meet the coming onslaught of heavy rain and crashing waves. "Damn! This one really caught us," he blurted as he looked to the chronometer, hardly seen in the low glow of the compass lamps. He peered... almost 2:30. He looked to the barometer. "Oh my God!" He then looked to the chart table. "How far out are we?" he called to Matt as he studied the chart of Chicago to Milwaukee.

"About twelve miles. We were doing well..."

"Yes, I know," a worried captain replied. The squall line now passed but with a building of strong gale winds and heavy seas in its wake. He used his right thumb and index finger, not bothering with the caliper, no time, to determine distance and to come up with a direction. "Take her to northwest by west... 325 degrees." The *Lady* dove into the now-oncoming waters cascading over her bow as she then rose high to dive again into the next onslaught now of eruptions with no sense of direction, lightning and thunder in a continuance that the captain could never remember seeing in all his days.

* * *

"Patrick! Patrick! Oh dear God in Heaven! What are we to do?" Molly Cooney cried out in Gaelic to her husband who was trying to calm his son as she hugged their daughter, as the family vied with other deck passengers in trying to find a safe refuge on the hurricane deck from the driving, biting rain and erupting waters.

"Och. It is only a common storm to these regions," Pat said, trying to minimize his own worries. "It will pass quickly. I understand they come and go in only minutes." A sudden drop to port threw he and John to the deck and they rolled together into the railing. John screamed in pain as the stanchion caught him in the lower back, then released him as the *Lady* rose again, heeling to starboard and they rolled back to where Molly and Nora were hunched together, using a guy wire to the smokestack as a support. He grabbed Molly's left leg and held John to his chest as the *Lady* rose again in a torquing movement to port, then dropped into a roiling trough only to rise again seeking another crashing wave, the rite of passage to Milwaukee now forgotten as they huddled and prayed as never before.

* * *

"Och! Oh my God! We are in another one of those storms!" Cecelia shrieked as the darkened cabin made a sharp drop to starboard, throwing Sarah Jane and she to the cabin floor into a pile with Fergus and George, the four in a mass of flailing arms and legs, reaching out and holding in a cabin of frenzy and fear.
"George!... George!"
"Fergus!"
"Oh Jesus! What in..."
"Sarah!"
"Cecelia!"
The *Lady* rose and dropped as she attempted to right herself and head into the oncoming storm, not abating but building with turbulent winds from offshore of Winnetka, ten miles distant.

* * *

Fred Ramsey, a proud apprentice wheelsman, finished his visit to the public toilet on the main deck aft of the starboard-wheel housing. He picked his way through the crowded deck of some sleeping, but mostly slumbering deck passengers all wanting to get back to Milwaukee as soon as possible. The moderately side-to-side motion of the *Lady* as it cruised along was suddenly pushed by a wind force from the northwest with a great howl to his left as Fred saw a wall of water highlighted by the now constant flashing of lightning and the rumbling of thunder, suddenly cresting along his limited horizon of vision. "Holy shit!" he yelled as the main thrust of the squall line coursed onto the port side of the *Lady*, causing a huge wave action to engulf the boat, then pushing it to starboard in a great roll, tipping all aboard into great pandemonium.

* * *

"Ah. Yes. Ladies and gentlemen! I have just received word from our captain that he wishes that we close our saloon's bar as he expects some bad weather and would wish you well in making preparations." Chief Steward Rice did his best to bring his captain's wishes to the still-roistering saloon diehards who seemed hell-bent on having a hell of a time all night if need be.

"It's only a little after two," a fellow in the uniform of a Green Yager griped. "It's early." The group he was with, a mixture of the various militias and others, clapped and hooted and shouted for more drinks.

The chief steward raised his hands and shook his head. Ah, it can be a bitch, he thought as he turned to his head bartender. "I'm about done in but they still want to play and if they play, they pay." He thought a moment. His cut from this trip was great. Hey, he made himself a bundle. Another half hour won't hurt. He looked to the clock on the wall behind the bar. Almost two-thirty. "I can give you until three o'clock. Then I shut down." He stood for a moment, feeling strange but with still-familiar feeling. "Oh... what the...?" he gasped, really knowing now, as the *Lady* made a sudden thrust to its starboard side, that some force beyond his understanding was now in control of the *Lady*.

* * *

138

"Whew. What a day!" Garret said to himself as he thumped his pillow, hoping to be able to get some sleep after a trying day, the cabin in darkness. He heard only the sounds of his son Will and his friend in their rhythmic breathing, both well into dreamland. Ah, yes. What a day! He lay in his bed fully clothed, except for shoes. He exhaled deeply and reviewed the events of the day, the effects of his having three whiskeys since midnight helping him into his feeling of euphoria. The moving of the rifles the first thing this morning... ah, they are safe, and tomorrow will be put into Fergus's mortuary's basement until we know when we can parade them. Or, he wondered... use them in a war? With whom? The United States as might Randall... or the South? And who in the South? Not all want to secede... And Fergus? I've never seen such a change in anyone as I have seen in him this day... Andy says he met a young lass who came in on the *Lady Elgin* and has really taken to her. Ha. He must be. I haven't had a chance to talk to him all day, except for the parade and earlier with the rifles. Oh yes. The parade. The men were great. It would have been even greater if we could have done our arms presentation routines... but we did parade, and in Chicago! A hell of a lot better than Milwaukee or Racine and everyone says they have enjoyed themselves... he chortled... even now. The room heeled slightly and returned to its slow undulations... And Douglas. What a man! What a great president he will make. He certainly knows his government and his speech was tough and right on the money.

The cabin room heeled again, now deeper as he then realized that more heeling was happening as the room rose and banked, to what direction he did not know, then crashed with a tumbling, the two boys and himself into a tangle in complete darkness except for faint traces of lightning flashes through the draped windows.

* * *

139

The *Lady Elgin*, her side-paddle wheels thumping, coursed eastward at a good pace. First Mate Davis finished his toilet and eased himself into his bed and gave a sigh of relief for the pain in his lower back easing as he settled in for what he hoped would be a good couple of hours of sleep. This damn back pain... it seems to be getting worse. But then he rationalized. Being on one's feet all day can cause some back problems... His thoughts flitted... Captain Wilson... Jack... retiring... so soon... so sudden. I wouldn't have believed it if he hadn't told me and his hoping I would get the command of the *Lady*. What a man. My God. What experiences he's had... but to what avail? Away from his home most of the year and all in the good times... and me. The first mate rolled into a more comfortable position, the pain easing. My Emma in Houghton with her seamstress work... she is content for me to be in and out on our stops there in the sailing months and then our long months before the fireplace. It is a shame we cannot have children, or we would have dozens. Ah, maybe hundreds.

He gave a yawn and in a few minutes he was sound asleep, lulled by the rolling *Lady* as she trailed twin wakes from her paddle-wheels eastward.

"Eh! What?... What the hell!... he tried to brace himself as the cabin tilted to starboard, then returned to port, only to tilt again to starboard more steeply. The first mate was thrown from his bed. "Damn! A squall!"

* * *

"Captain. I see a light."

"In this? My God. Where?"

Second Mate Beeman pointed through the rain-lashed window. He looked to the compass, moving erratically. "About dead ahead!"

Captain Wilson squinted, seeing no light. He looked to the chronometer... 2:35. The storm continued unabated with flashing lightning now showing a vessel, which he could now see, with a single bow light, bearing down on the *Lady*. He gaped at the looming hulk, a schooner as best he could determine. "Good God! She's coming right at us!"

His mind raced. I'm to take the *Lady*, according to the rules... what rules in a time like this! It's the best man for himself in most instances and now?... He knew he had to hold to port as a steamer with its own power. To hold and let the schooner, a lumber hooker he guessed, pass him to port or wait for us to pass in front of her. Damn!

"Captain... what? She... it's coming right at us...!" Marvin called as he and Matt fought the helm as the *Lady* now lumbered into the oncoming phantom.

"My God! They must see us. We are lit up like a Christmas tree. They have to see us," Captain Wilson shouted. "Take her to starboard. Hard!" he yelled as he pulled the bell for full speed. "She has to pass us to port... Damn!"

* * *

The *Lady* staggered as the bowsprit of the unknown leviathan knifed into her portside just forward of the paddle wheel housing, the severity shearing off the housing and the wheel, creating a huge gash in the hull which was now filling with cascading, turbulent waters. The two hulls held together for a few moments, then parted with the *Lady* still maintaining its northwesterly course erratically, the hooker slowing and following the main course of the winds to the southeast as being dragged.

"Captain!" Marvin called, the helm almost useless but with some control for the starboard wheel.

"Yes. I know. We have been hit hard. I must check to see what damage has been done." He stared to see the gaping hole where the wheel had been. "My God! The wheel is gone!" He turned to Matt and Marvin. "Do you see?" he pointed. "The port wheel is gone!" he gasped in almost disbelief. Then, realizing the storm was still upon them, he called, "Take her aground." He looked through the flashes of lightning and saw in the near distance cresting waves beating on the shoreline. Only then did he realize how close to shore they had been sailing. At least they were close enough to be able to beach. "We must beach the *Lady*." he called. "We must get ashore. God bless us all!... and the *Lady*."

Finis

EPILOGUE

Friday, September 16, 1860

The decayed and shattered body of Captain Wilson was found by fishermen three miles east of Winnetka, Illinois. He was identified by his watch and documents. His body was taken to Chicago.

Friday, September 21, 1860

The body of Fergus Kilbane of Milwaukee was found among debris of the *Lady Elgin* four miles south of Evanston, Illinois. He was identified by his wallet.

Thursday, November 8, 1860

Garret Barry's body, bearing many marks of injuries, was recovered by fishermen offshore of Gary, Indiana. He was identified later by his uniform of Captain of Barry's Union Guards. The actual number of souls aboard was never determined. Records indicate 298 bodies were found, but the total loss might have exceeded 400.

Thursday, December 20, 1860

A convention of the State Legislature of South Carolina on this date approved unanimously the first ordinance of secession which read:

"We, the people of the State of South Carolina in convention assembled, do declare and ordain... that the Union now subsisting between South Carolina and other States, under the name of the 'United States of America,' is hereby dissolved," making South Carolina a free and independent country.